JUNGLE QUEST INTRIGUE

JUNGLE QUEST INTRIGUE

A Romance

by

William Maltese

Writing as "Willa Lambert"

The Borgo Press
An Imprint of Wildside Press

MMVII

SECOND EDITION

1

Fear dilated Laura Lexly's blue eyes as she glimpsed snag-like treetops perilously close. Absentmindedly, she twisted an unruly strand of her short-cropped, sweat-saturated blonde hair that had lost all of its attractive beauty-parlor curl. She swallowed hard, and her mind flashed visions of horrendous disaster; no matter Jim Kenner's already proven worth at the controls of this small single-engine plane. Her stomach churned, giving rise to the nausea she'd barely controlled throughout most of her wild roller-coaster-like ride through the turbulence percolating upward from horizon-to-horizon jungle and from upthrusts of ragged stone.

"Jim's landings here are always a bit hairy," Kurt Reiger confessed, nervously chewing on his lower lip. His violet eyes, purple against the mahogany tan of his face, were dark with concern, and the deep dimple in his right cheek wasn't punched there by amusement. Anxiously, he ran his large and well-formed fingers through his thatch of cut-short curly black hair and, doing so, contributed to the tousle of interlocking strands.

Laura could see much of the boy-she-remembered in the man-Kurt-had-become. Although, calling Kurt a boy at fifteen, when Laura had last seen him twenty-four years before, was probably a misnomer. More to the point, Laura, eleven at the time, had been a girl: a slow bloomer who hadn't exploded into official womanhood until a whole year after the tragedy and after Kurt had been spirited away.

The air was suffocating in the cramped and super-heated confinement of the small plane and she felt like a sculpture of butter she'd seen in a magazine layout of Jean Winston's society wedding, neglected as it melted on a side table. Perspiration uncomfortably meandered her spine, her front, and her sides. She tasted salt whenever she licked her lips, and she licked her lips more often as the plane approached even closer to their hostile destination.

"There!" Kurt pointed through the bug-splattered windscreen. The clearing, thus identified amidst all those crags and greenery, wasn't reassuring. It looked too small for its intended purpose. If Laura were in a helicopter, or in any other aircraft capable of a vertical descent, she might, just might, give odds for a successful set down. As it was, she'd shut her eyes, since that had worked on takeoff. Unfortunately, she spotted Kurt's white knuckles instead.

"Jim hasn't skewered me on these treetops, or creamed me on these cliffs, yet," Kurt encouraged, and he released his death grip on his seat long enough to give Laura's knee a reassuring pat.

His touching her had been a spontaneous consolation offered by one nervous flier to someone who gave all outward appearances of being yet another. It had been as automatic as their hug upon meeting in Septiaola that morning, and it was given without any ulterior motives.

But Laura stiffened. She knew her mother would disapprove. The spectre of her mother's disaproval, all the while with her, had been given birth the moment Laura had even half-jokingly considered joining this expedition. June Lexly had already lost a husband, not only to this same jungle, but to the father of this same Kurt Reiger, and she insisted she couldn't survive losing a daughter in a similar manner.

Nevertheless, here Laura was, driven by her own demons, and, as her mother saw it, consorting with the enemy. Though, until Laura better dissected the ramifications of Kurt's even momentary return into her life, she figured it imperative she view any physical contact between them as less than welcome.

The plane banked sharply, and the continuing precariousness of the landing-in-progress made Laura wonder, and not for the first time, if her mother hadn't been right. She, Jim, and Kurt had deluded themselves when they believed they were going to make any kind of difference here, twenty-four years after the disastrous fact.

Jim's blond, tanned, green-eyed, and cooly confident demeanor at the controls might have reassured Laura of, at least, a safe touchdown; the plane's familiarly erratic engine noises might have done the same. However, like a drowning woman, Laura occupied herself with segments of her past: her childhood in Santa Fe, New Mexico; Karl, Elsa, and Kurt Reiger next door; Kurt and she at church; their fathers, Kurt, and she in the caves of Mesa Juanita; her father mailing postcards from cave explorations in France, Colorado, New Guinea, Tahiti, and, finally, lastly, tragically, Brazil.

The lowering of wing flaps sent vibrations through plane and occupants, and Laura was jarred back to the here and now, even though she preferred the escape of reverie. Their steep descent was into dangerous trees whose serrated edges extended an open invitation to impaling. Jagged, knife-like hunks of rock accompanied with similar invitations, and Laura tasted the danger.

Kurt took hold of her hand and squeezed, more for his own comfort than for hers. He detested flying, in general, and he suspected Jim was a sadist who could make flying under ideal circumstances seem scary.

"I loathe airplanes, especially small ones, particularly this one," Kurt said.

Laura was reading his lips: the squealing, squeaking competition from straining metal made normal conversation impossible. She did find his confession charming, if not at all calming. She had anticipated that this environment was tailor-made for men and that women needed to come across as invincible.

A battering-ram branch came so close to one window that Laura jerked back in fear of it coming through. She returned, pound for pound, the pressure of Kurt's continuing handclasp and willed herself to become part of the cracked and weathered cushions of her seat. She was further jolted by landing gear that touched and then tripped over rough ground. She managed a silent prayer and completed it as a wall of rock and shrubbery reared directly in front of them. At the moment before impact, the plane tilted noseward and converted the last of its momentum into a surprisingly graceful half-pirouette. Laura was left breathless and with a dull headache. She removed her hand from Kurt's, attributing the tingling that came with it to the momentary loss of circulation her fingers had suffered while subjected to his vise-like grasp.

"Well, if we've got the jello out of our legs, shall we disembark?" Jim cheerfully suggested after the plane became silent. He was in an obviously good mood, the least affected of the trio. He wasn't transplanted from Phoenix, where Laura now lived, or from Portland, like Kurt; instead, he'd been born and raised here in Brazil and he was acclimatized.

If Laura expected a reprieve from the heat and the humidity she'd endured in the aircraft, she was disappointed upon stepping outside. Mugginess greeted her with the subtlety of a sledgehammer. The impact took away what little breath she had left. At the same time, she smelled a musty, rancid earthiness that was more reminiscent of dying vegetation than freshly plowed fields. The complete trapping of sunlight by bordering stands of towering trees and rocky crags only magnified the overall sepulchral effect.

Her first impression was one of "something" out there: a thousand-beady-eyed enemy whose attention was focused entirely on her. At the same time, the already narrow perimeter of the clearing seemed to close in: warrior plants on the march to refill the momentary gap in their ranks as quickly as air jealously rushed to fill a vacuum, or as totally as darkness greedily swallowed any hint of light at sunset.

At that moment, Laura might have appreciated another reassuring squeeze of Kurt's fingers around her own, but instead she compensated with a shiver.

"What?" Kurt asked intuitively from close behind her, and he suspected his immediate empathy was a holdover from their shared childhood.

"Remenber when I got myself stuck in that crawlway in the Mesa Juanita caves?" Laura answered his concern with a reference to something they'd long ago shared.

"Of course," Kurt mildly chided. It was something he'd never forget. "Possible flash floods from unseasonal squalls in the desert; rangers bellowing for us to get out or chance drowning like proverbial rats."

"I was terrified," Laura reminded.

"We all were," he said, unwilling to grant her a monopoly on the emotion.

"Cold, pain, wet, fear," she reiterated. "Mainly the fear. A mile below ground, a girdle of solid stone anchoring me to the spot, and I never once imagined the walls and ceilings were closing in. All the caves I've been in since, all the tight spaces I've maneuvered, and I've never known an abnormal dread of confinement—until now."

This bracketing by shadow-filled trees frightened her. So, what had she expected? A picnic? Her mother had warned her, not only of Kurt but of the Amazon. In June Lexly's opinion, neither was a fit companion for woman, man, or beast.

"The claustrophobia will pass," Kurt promised and smiled encouragement and sympathy. It was a pleasant smile that further deepened the attractive dimple always evident in his right cheek, and it crinkled the laugh lines at the corners of his clear violet eyes. "You want to know *my* first impression of this place?" he asked, his smile converting to a mocking one. "Something, or somebody, out there watching me."

The invisible hair along Laura's arms began to stand on end. She wanted to ask if his paranoia had really passed, tell him his first impression had been hers, too, but she was interrupted.

"Ah, there they are!" Jim said. He'd exited the plane and secured the aircraft with block and tackle. Now, he pointed toward two young Indians, each in Khaki shorts and shirt, who had materialized from the underbrush and were headed in their direction.

The encampment was off the runway, reached by a short path through towering trees whose continuing undefined menace enhanced Laura's sense of ill-being.

The main tent was straight out of *The Arabian Nights.* it was a white conglomeration of canvas with three graceful arches that branched off a large central dome. "Man by the name of James Rommel designs and manufactures them in Israel," Jim said. "They look great, are easily set up, and are functional to boot."

The interior was spacious, the atrium a communal area, while the three smaller offshoots acted as sleeping quarters, Jim pointed out during the grand tour. "Unfortunately, we've only a short time to enjoy before Captain Fortuna-Mata is due to check in with our final go-ahead from the Brazilian government. After that, it's the great outdoors and hammocks hung from trees. You are still up to it, Laura?" Thankfully, it didn't sound like a dig. What it did sound like was an honest query from a man who not only figured Laura knew her capabilities but one who was willing to take her word for them.

"Ask me again later," Laura parried tiredly. After what she'd gone through to get this far, she just wanted to enjoy the luxurious accommodations that, at least for the moment, shielded her from jungle heat, jungle oppressiveness, and jungle eyes.

"A drink?" Jim suggested. "After which I'll lead the stampede to our bathing facilities."

Kurt collapsed in one camp chair, Laura in another.

"Unfortunately, it's a very limited bar," Jim apologized. "It's gin and tonic for me, and tonic for you two Mormons in our party. All without ice."

Laura found it inexplicably difficult to focus for long on what Jim said or did with Kurt around. Growing up, Kurt had been important in her life, and Jim was a new acquaintance. Now Kurt and Laura were resuming a childhood friendship. Not that Jim hadn't always been part of the total picture that brought Laura and Kurt together in the Amazon for this reunion. Like his father, Daniel Kenner, who had been the initial impetus behind the ill-fated first Kenner-Reiger-Lexly expedition, Jim was the one to suggest this get-together for the heirs apparent. As the children of the three missing men, they were undeniably interested in fitting together the pieces, old and new, that accompanied the mysterious disappearance of their fathers. Almost everyone else was dead or had lost interest, except the reporters who had written a brief flurry of news articles to accompany the recent discovery of the ill-fated expedition's last assumed campsite, all of these years later.

Laura's mother had had little, good or bad, to say about Jim Kenner or Jim's father. That was because June Lexly had known neither. Daniel Kenner had been an anthropologist who left Brazil only infrequently. He *had* been on hand for the opening of the Nitches Cave Complex in southeastern France, and he'd met and befriended Karl Reiger while conducting an exploratory survey of the deTwip Cave Complex in New Zealand. That was all before the Reigers met the Lexlys by becoming neighbors in Santa Fe; before Peter Lexly had converted Karl Reiger's family to the Church; before Karl Reiger had converted Peter Lexly and Laura to cave exploration, or, as those in the know called it, spelunking.

Although Jim was Daniel Kenner's son, Laura would have guessed his the Teutonic heritage, Kurt's as the Brazilian, not vice versa. Jim's blond hair was only a few shades darker than Laura's. Its deep leftward-sweeping bangs kept it perpetually hanging boyishly over his green eyes. Like Kurt's tan, Jim's was the kind blonds, in general, and Laura, in particular, would have died for. There wasn't a peeling strip of dead skin, a burn spot, or even a splotch of unsightly heat rash; Laura, if she followed true to form, would progress from lobster to variegated reds, culminating in an unflattering peel. Jim's hands were as calloused as expected on someone who spent long hours examining his extensive coffee and cacao holdings. Kurt chaired several space-technology conglomerates, and his hands were just beginning to heal and harden as a result of his recent time spent in helping to clear the jungle airstrip. Laura had been acutely aware of Kurt's new calluses when he'd forcefully gripped her hand on the flight in.

Laura's attention, back on Kurt, was met by Kurt's smile in response to her obvious scrutiny. "Excuse the staring." Embarrassed, Laura apologized. "I'm afraid I'm daydreaming."

"I was wondering if I'd sprouted a horrendous wart on the end of my nose," Kurt said with a good-natured grin. While Laura might have found him amusing, charming, and thoroughly attractive, she was dissuaded from doing just that by all the reasons her mother would have found for finding him otherwise.

"Whatever ails any of us can be cured by a nice, leisurely bath," Jim diagnosed after he'd drained the last of his drink. "How about it?"

Laura located a fresh change of clothing in the pack one of the two young Indians had brought from the plane. Jim was ready with towels.

At the stream, Kurt led Jim across the water to a more distant tributary and left Laura behind in isolated privacy.

She peeled away the layers of her damp and sticky clothing and descended slowly into a natural bowl of rock from which water was constantly flushed by the swiftly moving stream. The water was surprisingly cool and, while it wasn't glacial, was definitely a temperature geared for refreshing satisfaction.

Skittishly, Laura checked her revolver to be sure it was handy. More than anything, the gun emphasized that this wasn't *just* Laura Lexly, Bank Manager from Phoenix First National, taking another typical, ordinary, everyday, run-of-the-mill bath.

She luxuriated in the seductive combination of water and soap as she painted her skin with rich lather and washed away a burden of leadweight weariness along with the dirt and sweat accumulated since her last real bath at the hotel in Manaus. The sponge-baths she'd managed since then, on the three-day boat trip up the Amazon and up its tributary, the Tapaua, to Septiaola didn't count.

She imagined her present bath made cool by snow carted by runners from faraway Andean peaks, her soap scented by carefully crushed petals from dew-wet orchids picked that very same morning. It didn't matter that the real coolness of the stream was the result of flow through streambeds choked with shadows cast by gargoyle-like trees that siphoned all sunlight; nor did it matter that the soap wasn't a bar but biodegradable liquid, actually smelling slightly medicinal, in and out of its small plastic bottle. It simply all came together to provide just the panacea the doctor ordered.

When Laura worked up the second lather in her short hair and submerged herself beneath the water, she was confident that every bug and insect hitching a ride on her since Manaus was drowned and washed away. She couldn't have experienced a more purely sybaritic moment. Not since her baptism had a complete submersion left her so filled with a sense of genuine well-being.

Her contentment lasted the length of her bath and lingered throughout those leisurely moments required to emerge from the water, dry herself, and dress. She had just pulled on her last boot and stood to work her foot to a more comfortable fit when the mood of the moment was shattered as completely as fine crystal on crude cement. It splintered beneath the force of pure, unadulterated evil that seeped out of the surrounding jungle to engulf her as completely as any shroud.

"Ugh!" she responded: so seemingly real was the assault on her. It might as well have been a slap to her face because it was so palpably obscene that it left her feeling dirty despite the thorough washing and scrubbing that had immediately preceded it.

She was made physically ill by the possibility that someone

had been there, all along, watching from the shadows while she bathed unawares. She should have been more on guard, all forewarnings telling her there was nothing friendly about this alien terrain.

Her wary glance nervously swept the adjoining greenery, her intuition homing in like a pigeon to its roost.

Whoever it was, Laura was positive "he" was hiding in one particularly dense patch of inky shadow. Her blue eyes dilated in an effort to discern the blacker black within black that would better define him for her. For the moment, she thought she saw him. Or, was it merely the way the shadows of one tall bush combined with those of others to provide the semblance of a man among the trees?

She wished for her revolver, carefully placed so as to be available to her when she was in the pool, now inconvenient on its dry rock at the edge of the water. Not certain she would be able to fire it if she had it, she, nonetheless, would have had incentive enough to use it in demanding whomever it was step forward and be identified.

She took a tentative step in the direction of the revolver. A couple more steps, a stoop, and the weapon would be hers. In the meantime, she kept her gaze fastened on his shadow, determined to flush him out. She was taken completely off guard, therefore, by sudden movement behind her.

"Ah!" she exclaimed and reflexes swirled her toward the possibility of a surprise attack from the rear.

There was no doubt about this one being a man, even with his littleboy looks emphasized by short black hair and a flawless olive-skin complexion.

"I startled you," he understated in beautifully articulated English.

"Yes." She felt chilled even though perspiration was already beginning to stain her fresh clothes. With a hurried glance over her shoulder, she checked the shadows and sensed that whomever had been there was now gone. She turned back to her new threat as he took a step forward. In response, Laura stepped back.

"I'm expected, no?" he asked. His slight build and short stature added to the illusion of youth.

How could he be expected out here in the middle of nowhere?

"Captain Garcia Fortuna-Mata," he introduced. Had he actually clicked his heels? Yes. Heels on a pair of impressively polished boots. The boots went with the rest of a neatly pressed uniform that came complete with gold captain collar insignias that added even more credence to his being who he said he was.

"Yes," Laura said, her mind blessedly coming out of its mad tumble. "The local government representative?" she ventured, his final identification verified by her vague recollection that Jim had mentioned the captain being due.

"Exactly," he confirmed and, this time, closed the distance between them without Laura countering with a retreat.

He took her hand in his and bowed gallantly from his waist, lifting her fingers near his lips but he didn't actually touch them with his mouth. When he looked up, Laura saw the thickest and longest eyelashes she'd ever seen. His eyes were a deep chocolate and told her, more than anything, that here was a friend not a foe. A wave of welcome relief flooded through her.

"I'm Laura Lexly," she said, giddy by the way her emotions were flung this way and that as if riding nonstop on some out-of-whack amusement park ride.

"I know," he said, Of course he knew. It was his business to know. Then again, not even he was privy to everything, because he asked: "Is there something the matter, Miss Lexly?"

What did she say to that? Laura quickly ran through her alternatives and worried about seeming hysterical. As a city girl plopped down, quite literally, in the middle of a jungle, she had no real basis of comparison by which to tell whether or not what she was experiencing was natural paranoia that came with the territory.

Nonetheless, her gut-instincts told her she had detected someone in the shadows as real as Captain Fortuna-Mata.

"Yes, I'm afraid there might be something wrong," Laura reluctantly admitted. For the first time, she realized the captain, like Kurt, had a dimple even when he didn't smile. Laura was thankful he wasn't smiling mockery or amusement now.

They sat in canvas camp chairs while the two young Indians conjured mouth-watering supper smells over a nearby propane-fed camp stove and an adjacent open camp fire.

"About this certain someone or something," the captain said, and Laura wished she could speak Portuguese as well as he'd mastered English.

"Actually, I didn't *see* anything," Laura admitted. She was able to distinguish that in retrospect, although it had nothing whatsoever to do with her continuing conviction that there *had* been someone there.

Apparently, the captain was prepared to give her the benefit of the doubt. "We do have several alternatives, don't we?" he said. "An animal, for one. Your survival instincts, honed by sudden introduction into a potentially dangerous and hostile environment, might have overreacted to something as small and inconsequential as, say, a mouse."

"Or to something, say as big and as dangerous as a jaguar on the prowl," Jim volunteered in alternative.

"Recent foot traffic has driven most of this region's animals into less-frequented forest," the captain reminded. "However, yes, there's always the exception."

"How about the local native populations?" Kurt asked.

"All indication is that they've followed the animals," the captain reported. "Again, there might be exceptions."

"Dangerous exceptions?" Kurt probed, and with her eyes, Laura thanked him, because his question was one she'd wanted to ask but probably wouldn't have. Spotting a Peeping Tom in the underbrush was bad enough without her hinting he might have been a killer in the bargain. Her not asking the question, though, was probably irrational in the face of the several stone arrowheads found among the non-caucasian bone fragments at the recently located last campsite of their fathers, only a few-days' march away.

"As you possibly already know, there's been no reported incidents of inter- or intra-tribal hostilities in this immediate area for over ten years," the captain reassured. "Not since the Quanquans packed up and moved out. Destination unknown. I'd judge smugglers the more logical and dangerous possibility."

"Which brings us to smugglers," Jim insisted.

"Certainly, they can't be discounted," the captain admitted.

"Smugglers?" Laura queried, now curious.

"Skyrocketing profits on the world markets from illegal sales of clandestinely acquired archaeological artifacts has made Brazil a chief pipeline for black-market Incan, Chimuan, Mochean, Valdivian, et al, objects routed eastward over the Andes from countries of origin like Ecuador, Peru, and Bolivia," the captain explained. "Although, smugglers have been less blatant since our crackdown after the scandal surrounding AZ246-D."

"AZ246-D?" Kurt and Laura echoed in unison.

"A major archaelogical find located entirely within Brazilian borders," Jim obliged. As a Brazilian, he was obviously more up on his country's current events than either Kurt or

Laura. "It offered one theory as to where some of the Incan population disappeared after the massive sack of their Andean empire by Pizarro in the 1500's.

"Dr. Henreid Durnel, of London University, discovered it in 1982 and returned to civilization with several priceless gold objects excavated at the site. No one knows how many more such objects were carried off by the thieves who ransacked the area even before Dr. Durnel got out official word of his discovery.

"Nor was gold the only objective. Whole sections of glyph-decorated buildings were sawed up and carted away for collectors whose appetites have grown insatiable for anything South-American primitive."

"I'm stationed out here now mainly as a direct result of the world protest over the pillage of AZ246-D," the captain followed up. "It caused a decided loosening of purse strings both in my country and in adjoining countries that've suffered a drain of their archaelogical heritage for decades. Success of our efforts is best illustrated by the swiftness with which our troops moved·in to secure and isolate the area around the recently discovered ruins at the headwaters of the Rio Palma. Failure can be read in the multi-million-dollar-a-year profits still realized by certain Brazilian dealers specializing in the buying and selling of west-coast artifacts. However, I'm not aware of any smuggling activities presently being channeled through this area."

"Which doesn't mean there can't be *exceptions,* right?" Kurt queried, calling upon one of the captain's apparently favorite words.

"Of course, I'm more apt to be aware of large caravans," the captain confirmed. "Luckily, most smugglers see the advantages of shipping their contraband in bulk as overriding the disadvantages it gives them of us being able to spot them more easily. Substantial profits have always been needed to balance out the high risks and costs of moving any merchandise undetected over such great distances; an overhead here that includes mules, men, guns and payoffs.

"Now that it's official government policy to stop them, even more contraband has to be moved in order to cover increased operating expenses. As for the smaller operators, it's surprising how many of them fall victim to snitches within their own ranks now that we've an expense account sufficient to inspire love of our country's cultural legacy."

"So much for that old bit about there being honor among thieves," Kurt commented with satisfaction.

"Have I mentioned Sao Paulo Mining, Limited?" the captain asked.

"They're into smuggling?" Laura asked, and the captain's expression told her she'd missed the boat on that one.

"They're into mining," the captain said and somehow made that sound as if it hadn't been self-evident; Laura appreciated his effort. "I'll be happy to point out just where if someone would be kind enough to get me a map."

Jim got up and returned shortly. He laid a map of the area on the small table around which everyone moved his chair.

"They have an exploratory team here," the captain said and pinpointed a spot southeast of the Rio Teffe. "And here, nearer the Rio Catua. Neither of which puts them officially in our immediate vicinity. However, I understand they haven't been doing all that well in coming up with lucrative signs of paydirt, and it might have struck them as feasible to prospect farther afield."

"Which would give them incentive to stay out of sight?" Kurt asked doubtfully.

"Not necessarily, but if I had traipsed for days through the wild and suddenly stumbled upon a vision of loveliness in her bath . . ." The captain didn't finish the sentence. He didn't have to. The picture he painted wasn't one Laura found in the least pleasurable. She got gooseflesh just thinking about the time-lapse between her taking off her clothes and realizing there was somebody out there watching. Raised in church beliefs that saw personal modesty as a virtue, Laura found the whole scenario doubly distasteful.

"How about independent prospectors?" Kurt asked.

"Oh, we can certainly count on there being some of those out there, presently unaccounted for," the captain said, confirming even more possibilities for the ever-growing list.

"Is this the Amazon Basin or Grand Central Station?" Laura asked with evident frustration.

All three men smiled in appreciation of her attempt at humor. Laura found Kurt's smile particularly attractive, but unfortunately, she hadn't meant to be funny. She doubted she'd ever again feel as carefree or safe about bathing out here as she had before some creep had spoiled it for her.

"It's a shrinking world," the captain admitted. "Which puts people in a lot of places today where you wouldn't have found them last week, last month, or last year. It was just such an increase in foot traffic that brought the remnants of your fathers' last camp finally to light. A piece of missing expedition gear literally tripped over by a geologist taking soundings for S.A. Petroleum. Hopefully, the pluses balance the minuses, in the long run." He gave Laura a pleasant smile.

"What about the oil companies?" Kurt asked.

"No activity anywhere around here," the captain replied. "And it's safe to say I'd know if there were. We're pretty well-coordinated regarding major efforts to develop and exploit our natural resources. Besides which, geologists are pretty valuable investments that employers usually prefer we keep a ready eye on."

"Which brings us to what?" Laura asked. She suspected this had become nothing more than polite small talk before they got down to the more serious business of eating.

"Whoever it was, I suspect he's gone by now," the captain said. "If he saw you, he couldn't have missed seeing me, could he? And—" He motioned toward his troops bivouacked somewhere out of sight among the trees. "—he wouldn't have missed my men, either. He'll have thought twice about sticking around to make a further nuisance of himself."

"I see," Laura said. She knew there would be no major manhunt launched to find someone who might not exist except in her imagination, and she could live with that, but she didn't have to like it.

Kurt gave her a look that said he understood, and Laura tried to muster an expression that told him she appreciated his understanding. After all, what could he do? What could any of them do?

"Franco!" Jim called to one of the two Indians. "How goes the meal?"

"Almost," the man replied.

Everyone, besides the busy cooks, settled back in his chair. The main subject of conversation was seemingly exhausted, and there was silence all around, save for the crackling from the fire.

"I would have been prepared to blame one of those college students," the captain resumed to put the proverbial derailed train back on the track, "but Professor Denlick, who's in charge of that group, has it under stricter discipline than a military encampment."

"What college students?" Kurt asked.

Whether a prospector, a geologist, a soldier, or now, some college professor or student, Laura knew there was a pervert out there somewhere.

"A group from the Universidad de Asuncion," the captain said and sounded content to take up where he'd left off. If he had any official business to conduct elsewhere, he didn't show any big hurry to do it. "Botanists out looking for new plants to cure disease, or something. They're holed up in one of the caves at deNali."

"Caves?" Kurt and Laura chimed in perfect two-part harmony.

2

"I know what you're thinking," the captain divined, "but remember, your fathers were here to explore a supposedly extensive cave system." Obviously, the captain had done his homework. "The deNali caves can, by no stretch of anyone's imagination, be considered an interlocking network. They're individual holes in the ground, each having been gone over with a fine-tooth comb during the search for the expedition. Nothing found. Besides which, the distance between here—" He pointed to the deNali caves on the map. "—and your fathers' last campsite—" His finger slid to where Jim, Kurt, and Laura would be headed tomorrow. "—isn't a few-minute's stroll. At the very least, it's three days of very strenuous hiking."

For a moment Laura had hoped for a major breakthrough from just such a conversation as this one, secret caves suddenly coming to light after all these years. But it was wishful thinking! When their fathers had been reported missing, it hadn't been a fly-by-night undertaking launched to find them. Daniel Kenner,

Karl Reiger, and Peter Lexly hadn't been adventurers about whom no one cared. They had been well-known, well-heeled, well-connected, and well-respected members of their respective communities, the Reiger scandal making headlines only after rescue efforts were finally gearing down.

Conversation was momentarily interrupted by the call to a supper served on a tressle table beneath towering trees whose upper branches interlocked in an impermeable weave. The table was rustic and, while obviously hewn on the spot with no concession to aesthetics, admirably performed its function of supporting food enough for a harvest crew.

Jim pointed out the selection but spent little time on the scrambled eggs of the powdered variety, bread with a golden and flaky crust, peaches from a can, honey from a jar, jam from a tin, and Brazil nuts from a tree six yards from where they sat. Not so briefly, he extolled the delectability of wild pig baked all day in a pit lined with plantain leaves and with red-hot rocks, rodent capybara basted in its own thick juices, and, finally, bite-size pieces of succulent monkey meat on small wooden skewers.

"I can't eat monkey," Laura shied with a discomforting shudder.

She didn't say so, because it was her own particular hangup, but the very idea of eating monkey conjured macabre visions of cannibalism reminiscent of those once conjectured by one of the few journalists who hadn't jumped on the bandwagon to smear Karl Reiger's name and reputation. The reporter had put Karl Reiger, with the rest of the lost Kenner-Reiger-Lexly expedition, into the communal cooking pot of hostile natives.

Laura was able to put those horrible thoughts out of her mind, but only because the monkey meat in question was visually unidentifiable in its present state, and because Laura had been plagued by hunger pangs since Manaus. Unhygienic dining conditions on the boat trip up the Amazon and Tapaua had challenged even her adventurous spirit. And since meals on the trail, beginning tomorrow, would consist mainly of reconstituted dehydrates from plastic bags, Laura felt compelled to eat something now. She found the pig too "wild" tasting for her palate, but after initial misgivings, she liked the capybara's milder pork-like flavor.

Spooning another serving of clingstone peaches, she realized she'd never tasted better bread, better butter, better jam. She'd never tasted better eggs and fried potatoes. It obviously had something to do with being out of the common kitchen where such food might taste more ordinary. She'd first noted the food-tastes-better-on-the-trail syndrome when she'd begun overnight hikes in preparation for coming here. Beneath towering Arizona cacti and blue skies, Laura had seen common oranges become ambrosia, and nuts and raisins take on the delectability of a gourmet feast.

The captain expressed only initial misgivings that his troops weren't enjoying anything as sumptuous, and he continued to indulge an appetite that squelched Laura's fears that everyone who ate as much as a pig immediately took on piggy proportions.

"I've decided to send Corporal Beves and Private Paolo with you tomorrow," the captain said once he'd cleaned up his plate and opted for coffee. "None of us can know for sure just what Miss Lexly really saw, so we might as well be safe as sorry."

Laura experienced a flush of gratitude that had less to do with the addition of two more people to their party than it did with the thought behind it. Laura saw the captain's soldiers as his way of saying he hadn't found her an hysterical female who fantasized voyeurs out of every shadow.

"Thank-you," she responded warmly and flashed him the

kind of smile she usually reserved for men she was out to charm.

"I'm confident you'll get where you're going without incident," the captain insisted. He returned her smile with an attractive flash of his white teeth. "It'll help, of course, that Jim has already covered much of your route before you."

Neither Laura nor Kurt missed his cue, although, once again, Kurt was faster: "When did he do that?"

Jim looked ill-at-ease by Kurt and Laura's obvious surprise. "I assumed I'd mentioned as much somewhere along the line."

"Three September to thirty October, nineteen-eighty-four, wasn't it?" the captain ventured, wiping his mouth on one of the linen napkins Laura thought bordered on pretentious in their present surroundings.

"You have an excellent memory for dates," Jim complimented. "My mother had just died, her last words something incoherent about father. I came here determined to find what happened to him. I found nothing. Ironically, I had to have passed by the old campsite a dozen or more times."

"Actually, my memory for dates has little to do with it," the captain admitted modestly. "I merely reviewed your file."

"His file?" Laura asked, her query spontaneous.

"All bureaucracies thrive on paperwork," the captain assured. "Compiling it makes certain types of people think they accomplish something. In this instance, those same people assumed I was curious. Of course, had they bothered reading and/or understanding their own handiwork, they'd have known I met Jim on his first trip through."

"You have a file on each of us?" Laura devined and found the notion unnerving.

"And *yours* is extremely interesting!" the captain said slyly.

"Is she the beauty she appears to be?" Kurt asked, following the captain's lead. "Or is she something else in disguise?"

"My lips are sealed!" the captain insisted. "How would you

like it if I let drop to Miss Lexly about your wife and three children in — Portland, Oregon, is it?"

"Kurt's married?" Laura asked, surprised in spite of herself.

"Lies!" Kurt denied.

Laura felt relieved, but she couldn't imagine why, unless reclaiming aspects of Kurt and her childhood relationship somehow counted upon their both being single now. In fact, she should have been relieved to hear he was married, not vice versa. Her upbringing would have put a married man securely off limits. Not that his being single somehow enhanced his potential as an "available man," as far as Laura could be concerned. Laura's mother undoubtedly wouldn't have survived any kind of romantic entanglement between the two, and *that,* even if such a relationship were possible, would have kept Laura firmly in check. Laura loved her mother dearly and knew what June had been through. What's more, Laura was already made to feel guilty by the breach between her mother and her that had occurred as a result of Laura joining Kurt Reiger in the Amazon.

Still smiling from his little joke, the captain assured Laura that her file consisted almost entirely of forms and paperwork filed by Jim to get her into Brazil and cleared for the area. "Plus verification that you aren't knowingly affiliated with any individuals or organizations undesirable to the Brazilian government," he added. "Your file will, however, soon be made fatter by one page. Yes?"

Anticipating the nature of that proposed addition, Laura was apprehensive.

"Ah!" Jim sounded, his right forefinger lifted and pointed skyward. "I have it in the tent."

"Good company, good food, and good conversation has momentarily made me forget I should always finish business before pleasure," the captain said.

"Signing of the release form is merely a formality," Kurt assured Laura as Jim left to get it. "I think Jim wrote both of us it might be necessary?"

Yes, he'd written Laura as much, and she'd come anyway, but that didn't make her find this moment any the less disturbing. There was something very scary about a whole government, with all its many resources, being so anxious to disengage itself entirely from an undertaking.

"It's just another bureaucratic hurdle that doesn't signify," the captain dismissed airily. "From where does that come: something 'not signifying'? *Alice in Wonderland?*"

It rang vague bells for Laura, but she couldn't place a reference. She was never good at placing obscure quotations in context, and she didn't much care. Only in Russian novels did people know who-wrote-what well enough to quote painfully boring passages verbatim.

"Beats me," Kurt admitted. He smiled widely. "Do I look like a character in some Dostoevskian novel, or what?"

Not for the first time, Kurt had spoken Laura's very thoughts. As usual, his doing so made her feel as if his mind's ability to run a parallel course to her own insinuated a type of invasion of her privacy that could be just as unnerving, if not more so, than someone watching her from the dark. If she didn't know why she wasn't feeling as upset by his intrusion, as she did by the other, she suspected it deserved some careful and concise thought whenever she had the time.

"I heard that American schools were sadly slipping in their educational standards," the captain bantered and shook his head in mock disappointment in that no one had been able to come up with the answer to his query.

"You're the one who can't remember," Kurt reminded.

"And *I* happen to be a grad of Penn State," the captain informed and winked at Laura. "Which proves my point, yes?"

"Yes," Laura granted with a laugh and found his punch line well worth the circuitous buildup.

They turned in unison as Jim returned to hand a couple sheets of paper to the captain, one to Laura. The captain, also, passed on his two from Jim to Laura. "So, you can see it's a standard straight-forward release form, everyone having gotten the same," he explained.

The pages were identical. Jim and Kurt had each signed one.

"There's always such a flap when and if people disappear," the captain proceeded. "Not that we ever expect the worst, but this jungle has swallowed up more than its share of people in the past. It's your father's disappearance that have brought you three here after all of these years. So, if something *should* happen to you, my government would like to be sure that—How should I put this?"

"Your government has to be sure it's covered," Jim said.

"Yes," the captain admitted with an accepting shrug.

Laura remained alarmed that, as her mother had predicted, this jungle apparently had the potential to be as people-hungry, all of these years later, as it was in 1963. Even more frightening, the Brazilian government knew that too, compelled to play Pontius Pilate by washing its hands of the affair before allowing the maze of greenery to do with Laura whatever it may.

She wondered who there would be to look for her if she followed her father into oblivion. She had no husband and no children. Her mother was hardly up to the trauma of another loved one disappearing. She had already warned that losing Laura, especially under these déjà-vu circumstances, would put her in an early grave.

Laura, who had no intentions of dying before her time, had argued that what had happened in 1963 could hardly recur in this modern day and age. Yet, looking around her, Laura saw little evidence in support of her argument. Without the aura and accoutrements of civilization brought to this spot by the four of them, it might well have still been 1963. It might well have been 1863. It might well have been the dawn of time. She wished she hadn't so lightly circumvented her mother's warnings.

She signed, but her hand trembled as she did so. She wondered if there would be some question about the validity of such a shaky signature should the Brazilian government soon need to pull out the release form as positive proof that the poor missing-presumed-dead Laura Lexly had very well known what she was getting herself into.

She handed all three pages back to the captain, tempted to grab back her signed one. Was she really here, risking her life, in an attempt to find two, possibly three, dead men?

She didn't like this jungle. She didn't like all indications of what she was likely to find in it. She didn't like having it down irretrievably on paper that she had walked into all of this with her eyes wide open. She didn't like her constant recollections of her mother's warnings—about the Amazon and about Kurt Reiger.

"You're quite sure about this?" the captain asked and left the pages extended in his outstretched hand as if he anticipated Laura's reconsideration.

Was she sure?

"I'm sure," she said and surprised herself by sounding more convinced than she was.

"Well, then," the captain said and folded the papers slowly and put them into the inside pocket of his jacket. He came to his feet and gave a parting nod. "My thanks to you for your hospitality, and I'll save final good-byes for morning."

The only thing between Laura and their departure was the last of a very long night.

Restless, she got up and slipped on her robe.

The tent overhead, and the canopy of tree limbs above that, blocked off most available moonlight. There were degrees of darkness, however, and Laura's eyes adapted to this one. Actually, this absence of light was nothing compared to the ultimate darkness Laura, like her father before her, had encountered within certain meandering passageways and dome-vaulted galleries deep beneath the ground.

She easily maneuvered the gauntlet consisting of the backpack she'd wear in the morning, shadowy camp chairs, and a map-strewn table. She stopped before the semicircle of finely woven mesh that, halved by its now closed zipper, kept Laura securely inside. A lesser degree of darkness, trapped among tall trees and back-lighting the mesh barrier, silhouetted the myriad insects who clung to the outside of the tent. A hand-size spider, seen from bottom-up and reduced for Laura to shadow-play porportions, claimed an unsuspecting victim. Laura shuddered and feared a jungle that could devour her just as easily.

"You should be asleep," Kurt whispered, and Laura gave a startled half-strangled cry that caught in her throat and died there. Her fast about face made her dizzy.

"Speaking of sleep," Laura managed with some difficulty, "why aren't you in bed?"

She turned back to face the covered doorway, and she folded her arms, aware of her fast and furious heartbeat. Her veins raced with blood laced with the adrenaline injected by Kurt's surprise appearance.

They weren't touching, but they were within mere inches of doing so.

"What are you thinking about, out here in the darkness all alone?" he asked.

She was thinking how husky his voice was when lowered to a whisper. She was thinking about what her mother would think about what Laura was thinking.

"I was thinking how all of this might not give any of us the peace of mind we're after," Laura said instead.

"Second thoughts," he said; it wasn't a question.

"Not as long as there's the slimmest chance I'll come away with a certainty that my father *is* dead," she answered. "I'd welcome the certainty that he died in a cave accident in the Amazon Basin. It's having to live with the 'maybe's' that's so frustrating."

Kurt knew all about the frustrations of the maybe's.

"Is that what you think happened?" Kurt asked, and Laura strained to hear him. "They found their fabled caves, got in but couldn't get out?"

"Don't you?" Laura asked. How quickly he'd joined her in reacting to the assumed potential when the captain had mentioned the deNali caves where the college botanists were bivouacked.

"I'll settle for that," he admitted. "I'll even settle for their having been killed and cannibalized by natives, or eaten by wildlife. I'd settle for just about any fate imaginable, except one that paints my father as a monster out to cover his tracks. Because I remember him, you know? I wasn't too young at the time to know with certainty who and what my father was. And I tell you, Karl Reiger was a good, kind, caring human being, man and father. He had his faults, but they weren't of the magnitude, or of the grotesqueness, insinuated by muckraking journalists who took advantage of a real tragedy to run down the character and reputation of a man unable to defend himself."

Laura couldn't argue against Kurt having been old enough at the time to make a truly reliable and unbiased assessment of a loved one. She'd been younger than Kurt when her father had disappeared — and, to this day, she was prepared to defend to the death her father's good name and character. However, Peter Lexly's good name and character hadn't been tainted by world-wide headlines extolling the opposite viewpoint.

"Do you think my father killed them?" Kurt asked, and his question jolted Laura out of her reverie. It was a question she'd always known he'd ask, from the moment she knew she'd be meeting him again, but that didn't make her answer any easier. Her heart ached for this man whose father's misdeeds might well have included far more than just the deaths of Daniel Kenner and Peter Lexly; so very very much more.

She turned back to him in the darkness, her throat tight.

Kurt knew what Laura's mother believed, and Laura *was* June Lexly's daughter. Like mother, like daughter?

"Whether or not your father did or didn't kill two men or two hundred thousand has nothing whatsoever to do with whom *you* are, does it?" she said. It wasn't what he'd asked, but it was the best she was prepared to do at the moment.

He put one of his hands on each of her shoulders and held tight when she reflexively tried to step back in direct response to the deluge of emotional confusion that strangely accompanies such contact. To no avail, she flattened her palms against his chest to push him away. She felt his ribcage expand and contract as he breathed. The pulse spot on his powerful neck throbbed.

"Beautiful *and* diplomatic," he complimented and leaned forward to place a light kiss on her forehead.

When he turned her loose, her legs were inexplicably weak; she wondered how they even supported her weight. She wondered, too, as he left her, if she even had the strength to return to her bed. If she blamed her deteriorated condition entirely on the physical and mental expenditures she'd had to make to get where she was, she, nevertheless, wished — no matter how seemingly harmless — he'd neither touched nor kissed her.

It just wasn't fair: her headache, her stomach ache, her lack of coordination that left her unable to manage even the simplest slipknot on her backpack.

Jim gave her a funny look and diplomatically shooed her to the sidelines and out of his way. She leaned back in her commandeered canvas chair and shut her eyes, tired beyond belief.

She'd hardly slept at all the night before. For one thing, and she told herself, by far the more important, there were her lingering sensations of being watched. As if whomever was out there had x-ray vision that could spot her each and every move, inside or outside the tent. Apparently, the captain's assurances that the culprit had been scared away by the influx of military personnel hadn't held water as far as Laura's rampant paranoia was concerned.

She couldn't understand why she had to be haunted by shadows now, without any preview during all of those lonely nights she'd spent on desert trails in preparation for this outing. There were plenty of shadows in the Arizona desert when the sun started its dip below the horizon. There were snakes and all other manner of creepy and crawly things; the Amazon certainly didn't have a monopoly on those. She'd faced and dismissed coyotes that howled at the moon and owls that screeched rather than hooted. She'd turned under her fears, turned off the sounds of the night, turned over in her sleeping bag, and had turned her dreams to never-never land, not waking until morning, and she'd felt great in the bargain. Her only explanation was that no one had lurked in the shadows of those Arizona nights, where, here, there was a living, breathing something. Obviously, her psyche had the innate ability to distinguish between the two.

Her confrontation with Kurt in the early hours of that morning hadn't helped matters, either. She'd gone back to bed and had rehashed their whole conversation, over and over, and wondered if she'd handled it correctly. It wouldn't have done any harm to tell him she believed, one-hundred percent, that his father was innocent. Except, that is, the harm to herself in telling a lie. No, it was far better to have told him the truth. He'd have known she was lying anyway. Then again, he might have so much wanted someone, wanted her, to join the minority of those who thought his father completely innocent, that he would have accepted her little prevarication at face value and thanked her for it.

"Well, here we are," Kurt interrupted her thoughts and pulled up a chair to face her. *He* looked wide-eyed and eager. *He* looked rested. *He* looked handsome in his bush jacket, open at the collar, his blue handkerchief knotted around his neck. "You feel all right?" he asked, his sixth sense zooming right on target. However, no bonus points this time, since even Jim had seen, without ESP, that she was out of sorts.

"The excitement," she alibied. No lie there! It wasn't everyday a thirty-five year old woman prepared to hoist a thirty-five pound backpack and trot off into the forest primeval.

"You can still back out," he reminded and wondered if that's what he really wanted her to do. No matter the show he was putting up, it wasn't easy for him to be here with Jim and Laura. Especially with Laura, knowing as he did the way her mother felt toward his family, in general, and toward him, the last living Reiger family member, in particular.

"I'll be fine," she assured. Mainly, she was assuring herself; a bit of positive thinking never hurt anybody.

"Well, then, as soon as the captain shows with his blessings and with his military chaperones, we can be on our way," he said, and his large hands connected with his knees in a punctuating dismissal that drew Jim's momentary attention.

"Yo!" Captain Fortuna-Mata called and exited a small forest trail with two soldiers following closely on the heels of his spit-polished boots.

A few minutes later, he began a rundown of Corporal Jean-Michael Beves and Private Joe Paolo's qualifications: "Both crack shots, which should increase your odds of supplementing your standard diet with a bit of meat. I've tasted the dehydrated stuff." He grimaced and shook his head, then continued without mentioning the handiness of such markmanship for the purpose which brought the young men to the expedition in the first place; *that* apparently went without saying.

"Each as strong as an ox, which should come in handy in case any of you—" The captain didn't look at Laura. "—decide you're toting too much of a load."

"Looks to me as if they come with substantial loads of their own," Laura observed and nodded at rifles and backpacks temporarily shed and propped against a rock.

"Might as well be feathers," the captain boasted.

Jean-Michael cast a wide grin that revealed a gold-capped incisor. Laura thought the effect suited him but doubted few other men could carry it off as well. It was part of a face made surprisingly attractive by a clever blending of mostly imperfections. His eyes were set too wide, his lips were too thin, and his complexion was noticeably pockmarked. His eyes, however, were strikingly centered by inky pupils as dark as his naturally wavy hair.

Joe, in contrast, had heavily hooded black eyes and the facial features, complete with high forehead, high cheekbones, and large, hooked nose, of the stereotypical South American Indian. Laura had seen representations of ancient Mayans, carved on the walls of temples at Chichen-Itza, for which Joe might well have been the model.

"Both are staunch Catholics and happily married," the captain continued. "Corporal Beves has three fine children, the private has two." Again not looking at Laura, he hurriedly added something she barely caught about the folly of putting anything but tame foxes near a hen house.

"Last, but not least, Corporal Beves speaks Private Paolo's native dialect, Quilisijan, as well as English. Isn't that right, Corporal Beves?"

"Yes, I speak the English," Jean-Michael said slowly, his voice low and pleasant.

"Well, maybe not perfectly," the captain admitted and didn't make it patronizing, "but it can't help improve with practice. A person never gets the idioms and vernacular he needs from a classroom, does he?"

Laura could agree with him on that, from personal experience. She'd taken a crash course in Portuguese but still felt self-conscious when she spoke the language. Her every attempt, during her trip up the Amazon and Tapaua, to utilize what she'd learned, had been met by curious stares that had convinced her she might as well have been speaking Swahili for all the sense her listeners seem to make of her efforts. As often as not, the confusion had been cleared by somebody who knew enough English to be of assistance. Therefore, she appreciated Jean-Michael's situation and was determined to help him master conversational English. She felt doubly obligated in that neither Joe nor he would be along if Laura hadn't seen a man in the shadows; a man she couldn't help but feel was still there.

During the very first hour after leaving the campsite in charge of the two young Indians who had greeted Laura upon her arrival, Laura learned from Jean-Michael: "I come from small village on Rio Oyapak at Brazil and French Guiana border. I learn English from Catholic priest at missionary hospital. Wife, Maria, from nearby village. We now live Counani. Have daughter, Isabella. Two sons, Raol and Affonso." Laura even tried her hand at conversing with Joe but with less success. She couldn't understand his Quilisijan or Portuguese, he couldn't understand her English or Portuguese, and Jean-Michael showed no real inclination toward acting as interpreter; nor did Jim who seemed to have no difficulty conversing with either newcomer.

Laura's gleanings were less fruitful the second hour, but not because she was less interested or less determined. She found Jean-Michael charmingly unassuming, and she enjoyed coaxing him into stretching his usage of a language in which he was so obviously rusty. What did nip in the bud Laura's ready conversion to tutor, at least temporarily, was her eventual realization that her reserve of breath, needed to see her through her next step over twisted vines, around rotting logs, and through slippery rocks in swollen streams, was best conserved by keeping her mouth shut.

Through the rest of the morning, her conversation deteriorated to thank-yous whenever Jean-Michael was either there to save her from losing her balance, or was there to lend her a helping hand over the many trees that seemed to prefer falling over the trail rather than conveniently parallel to it.

"I'm jealous," Kurt said at lunch break. Laura and he were off to one side while Jim, Jean-Michael, and Joe, whipped up the midday meal with the help of two small camp stoves, each expedition member carrying a stove and a canister of white gas.

"Jealous of whom or what?" Laura asked curiously.

"I had visions of being Sir Walter Raleigh to your Elizabeth Regina. You know, throwing down my coat to get you across puddles? Offering to carry half your load. Even offering to carry you piggyback across tottering jungle bridges. Instead,

I've had to leave that to the corporal while I've had to contend with merely holding my own."

"Well, no need to be jealous," Laura consoled good-naturedly. "Jean-Michael is a happily married man, remember?"

"So the captain said."

"More to the point, he's a perfect gentleman," Laura insisted. "Or, as the captain would say—Something about tame foxes and hen houses, isn't it?"

"Caught that, did you?" Kurt asked with a warm full-bodied laugh.

"He did mumble it at breakneck speed, didn't he?" Laura recalled. "I suspect he was having second thoughts about its propriety, and rightly so." Her laugh was a gaspy reminder that she hadn't fully recovered from her morning walk. She blamed herself for not being in condition. Not that she hadn't made the effort, as all those Arizona trails could certainly bear witness.

By nightfall, she was literally ready to drop. She put up no arguments when Kurt suggested she spend the time remaining until supper in her hammock which had graciously been strung up for her by Jean-Michael. The extent of her exhaustion was best illustrated by the way she suddenly rationalized her continuing paranoia that someone was watching her from the sidelines: if he got his kicks out of seeing a woman collapsed and feeling as if she were breathing her last, then let him have at it!

She conked out immediately, and her companions took pity on her by letting her sleep. She enjoyed ten wondrous hours of blissful nothingness.

"I feel absolutely wonderful!" she exclaimed, emerging from her coma the next morning with a surge of energy that overwhelmed even the soreness of her muscles to propel her to an awaiting breakfast.

"I, on the other hand, feel lousy," Kurt said. "Why is that?"

He didn't look lousy. He'd shaved, his visible stubble of the night before gone. His square jawline was an open invitation for a woman's touch. But, Laura restrained herself and instead asked for a hot mush and raisins drowned in a pale concoction of powdered milk and hot water.

Day three saw her in relapse. It seemed she couldn't take a step without ending up in a hole, or tripping over a vine, or slipping on a stone. She was sure Jean-Michael would have probably expended less energy by hoisting her on his shoulders and carrying her all of the way, rather than his being continually there everytime she needed a hand.

By day four, she actually began to believe she may have finally found the natural rhythm that was going to get her through her ordeal. Granted, she hadn't greeted the morning with the same euphoric gusto with which she had greeted day two, but she hadn't been dragging, either. At lunch, she even had enough of her senses about her to realize what she was eating.

"No reflection on the cook, but is all of this beginning to taste the same?" she asked, spooning another glop of the paste the package insisted was chicken a la king. "What I wouldn't give for a good juicy steak."

"Meat?" Jean-Michael asked.

"Mmmmmmmmm," Laura confirmed, rolled her eyes, and licked her lips. "I could even eat a horse."

"How about a monkey?" Kurt chimed in.

That brought a chuckle from Jim and a shudder from Laura.

When they halted earlier than usual that afternoon, Laura was proud that she could have easily managed another couple hours on the trail; not that she was going to miss them.

"I figure we'll reach our destination sometime early tomorrow evening," Jim estimated.

His announcement left Laura unable to define her emotions. In less than a day, she would stand where her father had presumably stood on one of his very last days on earth. She preferred not to analyze her sinking feeling, nor how something Kurt's father had possibly done twenty-four years before was responsible for it.

"I'll cook supper," Laura volunteered, because she needed something to focus her thoughts elsewhere. Besides, she'd spent less time laboring over a hot stove than she'd expected. Granted, there was no big deal to hook up the stoves, light them, and pour the resulting hot water over freeze-dried food. Nevertheless, she felt it her responsibility to chip in now that she was up to it.

She collected the stoves and gas canisters and arranged them within the cleared area. The stoves were little different from the Whisper-Lite she'd bought for her excursions into the Arizona desert, so she had them set up and ready to go in no time.

"How about cocoa for our non-alcoholic apertif?" she suggested, after a check of her watch decided her it was a little early for their usual full-course evening meal. "Then, I'll get everything going for supper in, say, a couple of hours?"

"Sounds good," Kurt said, and Jim nodded in agreement. Laura managed to prepare the cocoa with ease. Everyone sprawled wherever convenient and sipped from aluminum mugs whose steaming contents seemed nowhere out of context in a jungle that steamed continual humidity in accompaniment.

Shortly, Laura sorted through the remaining selection of vacuum sealed food packages and tried to remember what had been eaten yesterday and the day before. It was difficult when one reconstituted meal tasted so much like any other.

"How about 'Chinese Delight'?" she suggested and turned with that uplifted package in hand.

"Ugh!" Kurt and Jim obliged with a mutual groan.

"How about meat?" Jean-Michael suggested in alternative.

"By all means," Laura agreed. She shut her eyes and joined him in what she assumed was light-hearted fantasy. "We'll have prime rib, pink and tender; mashed potatoes, fluffy and crater-filled with melted butter; asparagus tips, emerald-green and firm to the touch." Two things stopped her from continuing: one, the realization she was beginning to salivate; two, the begging of Jim and Kurt for her to have mercy.

"Sorry, Jean-Michael," she apologized, "but it looks as if 'Chinese Delight' wins the day, after all."

When he picked up his rifle, held it above his head, and proclaimed, "Meat!" yet again, Laura wasn't the only one who got the message.

"I do believe he *does* mean meat," Jim said.

"Suddenly, I know how and why all primitive societies held their hunters in such high regard," Kurt said appreciatively.

"Amen," Jim agreed.

There was no denying she would relish a change in menu, but Laura felt safest when they were all together. If she'd become more successful in shoving to a back burner her paranoia of being watched, there was no denying her sense of apprehension had a nasty habit of spilling over, like now. She wásn't thinking entirely of her own safety, either. She didn't want anything happening to Jean-Michael. If whatever was out there had been surprisingly benign, so far, intuition told Laura it was just waiting. For what or why it was waiting, she couldn't begin to fathom.

"He's a crack shot, Laura," Kurt reminded. He sensed her feelings and had moved to reassure him. He'd never denied her suspicions that they weren't alone out here in the middle of nowhere, and he wouldn't have been so easily persuaded to let Jean-Michael go if not for the prospect of savory capybara steak only a quick gunshot away.

"Yes, I'm crack shot," Jean-Michael agreed without coming across as an egotistical boaster. "You get firewood; I get meat."

Laura's stomach felt funny, and not because she anticipated any change of diet. An inner voice told her to use all of her wiles to convince Jean-Michael that "Chinese Delight" was better for all of them. Nor was she pleased how it might have been her comments on the tastelessness of the food, that noon, that had been the catalyst to bring Jean-Michael's provider instincts flooding to the surface.

"Jean-Michael, I . . ."

He didn't hear her. With a throwaway line to Joe, probably to let his fellow soldier know where he was off to, he'd been swallowed by a gaping maw of jungle greenery.

"It's been three hours," Laura reminded them nervously. She half-heartedly added another stick of dry wood to the stack collected for a fire.

"Remember the capybara and wild pig we ate the night of your arrival?" Kurt asked, determined to ease her mind if he could. "Remember the monkey?" he added with a grin. "Well, Jim and I spent a whole day and a half traipsing through jungle, much like this, before bagging all three in less than one short hour. It's a question of luck, with no guarantees Jean-Michael is having any, especially since most of the animals have made a mass exodus to less frequented stomping grounds. I sure haven't seen all that much wildlife these past few days, have you?"

"We shouldn't have let him go," Laura said, because it wasn't four-legged animals that concerned her; nor had they ever. "It's getting dark."

"Then, we'll be sure to see him shortly," Kurt assured. "He won't be doing much hunting after nightfall."

On cue, a gunshot sounded, muffled by forest underbrush.

"Ah, just taste that delicious capybara steak!" Kurt said with relief. He'd found Laura's sense of gloom and doom disquietingly catching.

Laura's instincts were less optimistic. Vigorously, she rubbed her hands up and down her upper arms to increase circulation and fight the chill that had nothing to do with a drop in temperature. In no way did she do so in any conscious invitation, and she was genuinely startled when Kurt's arm wrapped her shoulder and he gave her a quick hug.

"Why did we let Jean-Michael go?" she asked. At the same time, her chill returned with a vengeance, and she wished she had Kurt's physical comfort again. His arm had felt warm. It had been comforting. It had felt good.

"Because Jean-Michael is as ready for capybara steak as any of us," Kurt said, and he didn't use her latest bout of shivering as another excuse to offer his arm. He wasn't sure why he'd offered it the first time, unless he was subconsciously out, once again, to define her obviously guarded feelings toward him. If she was far less hostile than he'd been led to expect by all his mother had told him about the extent of June Lexly's adamant hostility, he continued, nevertheless, to sense Laura's inherent leeriness around him, and, despite all logic, he resented it. "Jean-Michael is probably the best shot among us," he continued and told himself that he shouldn't blame either June Lexly or Laura for whatever their feelings toward him, because Kurt, himself, still harbored his own fair share of doubts about his father's innocence; no matter what he'd told Laura. "Jean-Michael is the one most familiar with the territory. The best reason of all: despite whatever premonitions you and I might have, there's no hard evidence to support them."

"We would all be better in a helicopter," Laura reflected. "Fly in, set down, look around, and get out."

"Maybe," Kurt conceded but didn't believe it. "So, why did

we rule against one, I wonder?" He knew she knew the answer, but intuitively he sensed she just wanted to fill the time until Jean-Michael was, once again, safely among them.

"For one, there was the problem of fuel, wasn't there," she said; that it wasn't really a question assured him she hadn't forgotten any of the pros and cons he was sure Jim had written both of them. "For two, she continued, "something about distances and air time."

They walked, the irony of which didn't escape either of them. Since they'd spent most of the last few days begrudgingly on their feet, their leisure time would, more logically, have been spent sitting. Except, there was something therapeutic about a stroll which neither was required, by necessity, to make.

"Then, there's this wretched terrain, right?" Kurt reminded. "Even now, we're walking on a slant covered with trees and underbrush, rocks and gullies. We were lucky for a runway only a few days away. Luckier yet in that the runway was used just last year by a geological team; which meant we only had to clear off a year of new growth, not centuries of the stuff. I can tell you from experience, we were lucky not to have started from scratch."

Kurt had parachuted in with Jim to do the clearing that made the old runway serviceable. Jim and he had decided blasting trees, chopping undergrowth, and burning the results was better left to them, but it was only a last-minute crisis at the bank that had kept Laura from contributing to those preliminaries.

A parrot screeched: another welcome distraction. Its brilliant plumage was visible in the failing light, gliding on the same dangerous updrafts that, like so much else, had decided everyone against a helicopter. Until after sunset, air, heated by sunlight against the exposed faces of the many cliffs in the area, rose skyward to cause unpredictable turbulence the likes of which had been experienced on the flight in. Just such a cliff suddenly dropped away beside the pathway where Kurt and Laura paused to take in the fading view.

Night would make it ever so easy to misstep over the brink into oblivion. Below, there stretched more undulations of endless twilight-darkened greens, punctuated by gigantic up-thrusts of rugged rock that hinted of geological upheavals in times past. No one in his right mind could find this beauty friendly.

"This way, we come in at ground level, better able to spot the clues," Laura said and sounded like a schoolgirl delivering a memorized dissertation. Her superfluous litany emphasized her continuing need to fill time and space with small talk. "We couldn't count on spotting clues from the air, could we? Case in point: the geologist who stumbled on our fathers' last campsite did so by hiking through the bush, not by flying over it. Point two: the jungle is 'The Great Eraser.' In the blink of an eye, it wipes clean cities, runways, and campsites, and it replaces the lot with huge trees and dense underbrush that makes clues best detected from close-up.

"Then again, how many times, these last few days, might there have been a clue only a few feet away that I was too tired to see it, or too intent upon putting one foot in front of the other to care about anything but my own survival? I'm no more able to spot clues here than I would have from the comparative comfort and safety of a helicopter."

"Maybe that was the case for the first couple of days, but now?" Kurt argued in compliment to both their abilities to cope better.

"Hello, you two," Jim interrupted and joined them on the edge of the precipice. "I have some good news and some bad news."

"Let's have the good news, please," Laura insisted. She really doubted if she were up to the bad.

"As good as his word, Jean-Michael has returned with meat for the larder," Jim announced.

"Fantastic!" Kurt exclaimed, relieved that Laura's dire prophesies were wrong and delighted at the prospect of fresh meat.

Laura's relief was a palpable wave that flushed through her. Why did she see bugbears and disaster at every turn?

"The bad news is that he's bagged a monkey," Jim volunteered.

Laura's laugh was more than a little hysterical. Of all the horrible things she'd fantasized, the reality was this! On the other hand: "I can't eat monkey," she said and, for not the first time, shivered at the thought.

"Seems Jean-Michael doesn't know that," Jim explained, his smile in contrast to his attempt at seriousness. "He wasn't around, remember, when you turned up your nose at monkey meat. I think he may even have misinterpreted our laughter this noon when you suggested you could eat a horse, and Kurt substituted monkey. English idioms and vernacular are always difficult for someone learning the language." The last was paraphrased, with a smile, from what the captain had said earlier. "Right?"

"Maybe if you shut your eyes and pretended it's something besides monkey," Kurt suggested. He wasn't taking it seriously, either.

"I did that the first time," she admitted, "and succeeded only because it was disguised as little chunks."

"Well, it admittedly wasn't disguised in little chunks when I last saw Jean-Michael skinning it for the skewer," Jim confessed.

"I do see the possibilities for humor in this," Laura admitted and decided to spell out what she probably should have explained the first time around. "Unfortunately, it goes deeper than my just being a particularly finicky eater." Jim and Kurt's features were barely discernable in the same darkness, but she had each man's attention. "When I was in high school, I came across some old newspaper clippings about the disappearance of our fathers. One particular article went into some pretty grisly conjecture."

"A lot of them did," Kurt could only agree. He'd sorted through all the newspapers, too, and noted the atrocities they'd leveled at his father.

Laura, though, wasn't talking Karl Reiger, nor the monster he may or may not have been. "About the Quanquans," she clarified and hoped her reference to the Indians in the area when their fathers had come through was enough for Kurt to pick up on. She wasn't disappointed.

"In their role as cannibals?"

"And monkeys looking human?" Jim came in a close second.

Laura grimaced as smoke from the unseen, but obviously roaring camp fire, wafted through the shrubbery and enhanced her vision of what that long-ago reporter had speculated as to the fate of the missing explorers. "I can't help but associate the two," she admitted. "I didn't mention any of this before, because I somehow thought it wouldn't come up again."

"So, which of us tells Jean-Michael he's suddenly the only one eating his kill?" Jim asked without laughter. Laura had dreaded their mocking the truth, because she still hadn't convinced herself her revulsion was completely logical. After all, monkeys were no more human than rabbits were cats, and Laura enjoyed hasenpfeffer, no matter what the bunnies looked like dressed out and hanging in a butcher's window.

"How about the one who first comes up with the Portuguese equivalent for 'finicky eaters'?" Kurt suggested.

Both men looked at Laura, but she wasn't volunteering. If

Jean-Michael had killed the monkey because Laura had so loudly wished for steak, he'd expended a good deal of time and effort on her behalf. No matter the innocence behind her initiating his hunt, she felt a little guilty that she was now going to have to spurn his well-intended contribution.

"How about if we play it by ear?" Jim suggested. "Surely, one of us will come up with a diplomatic something."

"Like you distracting him while I chuck poor Mr. Monkey under the nearest log?" Kurt volunteered.

"Or some such other improvisation," Jim assured but not very convincingly.

With a reluctant Laura in tow, the two men joined Jean-Michael at the fire. The monkey was skinned and on a spit, and Laura thought she was going to be physically ill when she saw it.

"Easy, Laura," Kurt comforted and locked her elbow with his hand in welcome support.

Laura wasn't going to pull this off with anything like the aplomb she'd hoped for. She had to explain to Jean-Michael, since it was solely her problem. He wasn't stupid and was undoubtedly sympathetic enough to understand.

However, she didn't get the chance for explanations. He interrupted with a forefinger to his lips and a staccato hiss that demanded silence. He crouched at the edge of the fire and looked feral in the lighting that danced shadows off his features. His head cocked and his nostrils dilated like a carnivore sensing prey.

"Someone," he whispered.

"Something out there?" Jim asked. He unsnapped the flap of his holster.

"Some*one*, I think," Jean-Michael emphasized, and the finality shuddered Laura from head to toes. "Stay here, please!" he insisted.

After a typical parting comment to Joe, he was gone into the unfriendly night, and Laura hadn't managed, once again, even one strangled word of warning to stop him.

3

If push came to shove, Laura figured it should have been a foregone conclusion that Jim, not Kurt, accompany Joe to look for Jean-Michael. It was Jim, after all, who had been over this route before. Laura refused to accept that Kurt was going as the result of an "equal-opportunity" coin toss, especially when Jim and Kurt remained adamant that Laura, in this particular instance, should be excluded from the selection process.

"I think we should stick together," Laura argued, deciding *that* was the best course of action yet. She didn't want anyone else disappearing. Nor did daylight assuage her fears, especially since everyone had intermittently called to Jean-Michael since the first hints of sunrise, getting little for their efforts but echoes off rocks and screeches of monkeys. In truth, Laura found the jungle as ominous in day as in night; maybe more so: these unsettling trees that kept ground level in perpetual twilight.

"Joe and I will just make a quick reconnaissance," Kurt assured and pocketed the coin he and Jim had flipped for a win.

Laura thought "win" a misnomer, and she was little consoled that, like her, Joe had had no say in the matter; he had automatically been conscripted for the search party.

Of course, they were all against the four of them, in tandem, searching the bush. It would be slow and cumbersome, and it would alert the enemy—if there were one. More practical would be to divide up the immediate area into four sections, one for each to search. That, however, was dangerous from a divided-we-fall theory of warfare, and Laura didn't doubt this was war. Intuitively, she suspected Jean-Michael had unwittingly become the war's first victim.

"We have to make the effort in case Jean-Michael is down and needs assistance," Kurt superfluously reminded them all of their moral obligation.

"Maybe we should reconsider use of the radio Jim lugged all this way," Laura suggested, not for the first time. She had wanted to put the radio into service from the moment she'd felt certain Jean-Michael wasn't coming back, but she'd been overruled then and was overruled now.

"We don't know for sure that anything has happened to Jean-Michael," Jim reminded. "Until we do, what exactly do we radio the captain?"

"We radio him that Jean-Michael heard someone, went after that someone, and hasn't come back," Laura spelled out for him. "The captain can send some of his men, better equipped than we are, to conduct a thorough search."

"And if Jean-Michael suddenly shows up after we've radioed for help?" Jim asked.

"If the captain isn't already here, we radio him the good news."

"Then if something really bad happens farther down the trail?" Jim queried. "You've heard the one about the boy who cried wolf?"

"Something has happened to Jean-Michael," Laura insisted. "I feel it in here." She placed her hand on her stomach.

"If Kurt comes back with nothing, we'll radio," Jim compromised.

"*If* Kurt comes back," Laura ventured in pessimistic alternative.

"Look, I'll make all sorts of noise if anybody tries anything funny," Kurt guaranteed, grateful for Laura's ongoing concern but determined to make the effort.

"How many noises did Jean-Michael make?" Laura wanted to know. She felt as if she were banging on a brick wall. Not that she didn't understand where Jim and Kurt were coming from; they were this close to being where they wanted to be, and they didn't want to foul up anything now by radioing the captain about a *maybe* tragedy. The captain might radio back for them to stay put, or, much worse, to get out of there. Those signed release forms, absolving the Brazilian government of all responsibility, would be seen less favorably by the world press if word ever got out that the party had radioed in about trouble, and the captain let the three stick around to face it.

Laura wanted to reach their destination as much as anyone. However, the bad vibes she'd had for a long time weren't going away.

"If Jean-Michael is injured, and we do nothing until the captain gets here, he could end up dead when we might have saved him," Kurt said.

Laura didn't want Jean-Michael dead, but, more than that, she didn't want Kurt dead, either.

"Kurt is right, Laura," Jim agreed.

"And I suppose majority rules?" Laura asked in angered frustration. If anything happened to Kurt, she wouldn't forgive Jim his deciding vote. "So, do what you please!" If Jim and Kurt wanted Kurt to risk his life, so be it!

Kurt, though, didn't immediately respond to his hard-won dismissal, because he had something to say that it was important Laura hear and understand: "The chances of our finding out what became of our fathers becomes less if the captain suddenly orders us out because of what has happened, or rather, what *may* have happened to Jean-Michael," he said. "The bureaucracy may never allow us back, even if it's a false alarm."

"If I were you, I'd still take that chance," Laura insisted. Suddenly, she was a firm believer in the better-safe-than-sorry school of philosophy.

"I don't think you mean that," Kurt had the audacity to contradict. "You must suspect how the accusations leveled against my father affected my life. You surely see the potential that they have for affecting what life I have left." He was irritated that she pretended not to see. Her own way of relating to him had been tainted by those accusations against his father.

"You're not your father!" Laura drummed home. It took all of her willpower to keep from banging her fist against his impressive chest to vent her fury at his not being able to separate the two. "If I can make the distinction, my father being one of your father's possible victims, why can't you?"

"Because some people sift evidence better than others, basing their conclusions on facts," Kurt said and wondered just how unbiased her lifetime with her mother had really left her, "and others are too lazy to ferret out the facts, or are content with circumstantial evidence, or are governed by purely emotional responses that don't allow them to see beyond what they want to see. If Jim and you are among the fact-finding contingent—" And he wasn't one-hundred percent convinced they were. "—what of those others, like your mother?"

"What does my mother have to do with this?" Laura asked.

"I want the things that make life worth living," he said. "I want a wife, children, and a home. If I don't have illusions of that being an easy row to hoe, I at least want the chance to meet and overcome the obstacles without more cards stacked against me, by people like your mother, than are stacked against the ordinary guy on the street."

"So, I'll pray for your safe return," Laura frustratedly conceded, and, wishing she hadn't conceded, she made good her promise as soon as Joe and Kurt disappeared into the same greenery that had swallowed so many people before them. As she did so, she heard rain starting to fall into the canopy of treetops. The resulting drizzle soon drenched everything below—Laura included.

Jim began pulling their equipment under the protective umbrella of several large-leaf plants, and Laura joined him. She was surprised and jealous that he, in contrast to her, looked like a guest at a posh lawn party who'd sought temporary shelter within a charming garden bower.

"Why don't you look as put-upon by all of this as I do?" she complained, her momentary resentment showing through. "Don't you know that misery likes company?"

"Do you look put-upon?" he asked good-naturedly. "You could have fooled me."

"Tell me," Laura said and dramatically tried to fluff hair that humidity, and now rain, put beyond fluffing, "would you invite this home to meet your mother?"

Jim smiled. "You look fantastic!" he flattered. "If I weren't engaged, and Kurt and you didn't seem to have an affinity for each other, I'd come on to you like a bear to honey."

"Kurt and I have what?"

" 'No!' she doeth protest?" Jim asked but didn't seem all that repentant. Which Laura found downright disconcerting. Granted, even she recognized a certain "something" at work between Kurt and her, but, considering the two weren't complete strangers, that was to be expected. If Jim had misread and misinterpreted, she could easily set him straight.

"When Kurt and I were younger, we lived next door to each other in Santa Fe," Laura reminded. "Our families were friends. This thing with our fathers gummed up the works. My mother is still bitter."

"Were we talking about Kurt and you, or about Kurt and your mother?" Jim infuriatingly wanted to know.

"I'm my mother's daughter," Laura assured. "We're close." She didn't mention the monkey wrench this expedition had thrown into *those* works, because she was confident her mother's and her relationship was strong enough to survive the temporary schism — if Laura could only survive the trials and pitfalls Jim, Kurt, and this jungle put out for her.

"I see," he said. But did he see what Laura expected him to see? His you-can't-fool-me smile wasn't encouraging.

"So, you're engaged," she said. "Your financeé approves of this?" An airy wave of her hand and arm encompassed the whole Amazon Basin.

"Actually, yes. She has a strong sense of family," he said and fished in his pack for a Granola bar.

"That's your cue to pull out her picture," Laura encouraged.

The rain suddenly stopped, except for frequent drops from the still-saturated leafy umbrella. A slash of brilliant sunshine somehow penetrated the maze of interlocked tree limbs to spotlight an orange-lipped orchid couched within the forked branches of a nearby tree.

"Come on, Jim!" Laura cajoled when he didn't produce the picture as quickly as she thought he would. "There isn't a man worth his salt who doesn't carry at least one snapshot of his lady-love."

Granola bar held between his teeth, he produced his wallet of water-resistant canvas. Its Velcro seal made a distinguishable ripping sound as it opened.

"Sarah Naomi Ruth Judith Maxwell," he identified the girl in the snapshot. She was young and pretty, in a wrinkled blouse and dirty trousers. A checkered bandana concealed her hair except for a few carrot-orange strands that tumbled over her forehead. She was barefoot in a plowed field of . . .

"Potatoes?" Laura suggested, although it wasn't the vegetables or the girl that had her main attention. A background construction rose above the upturned field.

"That's where we met," Jim said. He looked like a man in love, even as he took another bite of his Granola bar. He sounded like a man in love, too. "In a potato field."

"In Israel?" Laura asked. It could have been elsewhere, but she only had her experiences upon which to draw conclusions. She remembered just such a tower in just such a field. Her Israeli guide had explained its function: "For when the enemy decides to move his tanks up to the border and take potshots at farmers and farm equipment. Spotters in the tower see them coming and give forewarning to get out of range." Laura waited for Jim to confirm.

"On a kibbutz just north of Metulla," Jim said, although it seemed a surprisingly reluctant confession. Laura couldn't decipher the strange expression on his face as he finished his Granola bar, took back the picture and returned it to his wallet, but what he said next did a good deal to explain: "For the record, I never believed that garbage about Kurt's father, but it might be better if we didn't mention to Kurt about Sarah being Jewish. It's an unnecessary variable, so why introduce it if there's even the chance it might complicate or compromise our existing relationships? Yes? It's why Sarah decided to stay away."

"And what did your mother think about Karl Reiger's supposedly nefarious past?" Laura asked. Laura's mother had certainly never spared her two-cents' worth.

"She never believed it, either," Jim insisted.

"Well, as I said, my mother believes it all," Laura said. "As far as she's concerned, Karl Reiger betrayed us and our church. She found his betrayal additionally galling, because dad, at one time, had taken so much pride and satisfaction in introducing the whole Reiger family to Mormonism. The newspapers never failed to remind everyone that Karl Reiger, possible Nazi butcher of Jews, and possible murderer of your father and mine, was a member of the Latter-day Saint church."

"And did you ever tell me what *you* believe?"

If she hadn't, she was willing to give it a try now: "At first, I doubted it could be true. After all, I knew the Reigers. What's more, I liked them. Karl Reiger was almost like a second father. Later, I gravitated toward taking everything my mother said as gospel; how could she hurt so much, for so long, if it wasn't all true? Still later, I went over the old newspaper accounts myself and decided the only thing seemingly all that positive was that Karl Reiger was German, a rocket scientist, and he was brought to the U.S. by our government after the war. I couldn't find any direct link between Karl Reiger, German scientist, and Karl Reiger, Nazi butcher who sent two hundred thousand Jews, gypsies, and romanian freedom fighters to extermination. Were there two Karl Reigers? Was the attempt to make them one and the same merely hype to sell newspapers? I only know our fathers disappeared. Your father and mine into jungle graves? Kurt's father into hiding in Paraguay, Uruguay, Argentina, or Chile? All three into a cave complex that swallowed them and never spit them out?"

"The cave theory can certainly be argued by forensic reports that put only dead porters at the last campsite," Jim conceded.

"Our fathers already lost in some cave when the porters died?" Laura completed the conjecture.

"A pity no one ever got any information from the Indians,"

Jim shook his head. "Closed-mouthed, the whole lot of them!"

Although it had been gone over countless of times, Laura found comfort in discussing it again.

"Why would the local native population have considered the cave complex sacred? It's hard to believe natives were sworn by oath and blood ritual to secrecy."

"There were certain references that might well be interpreted that way in notes my father left behind."

"Your father having had ready access to native secrets?"

"He was Brazilian-born and had an early association with several Brazilian tribes, because his father was busy carving a coffee and cacao empire from areas as primitive and as forsaken as this one. My father spoke Quemcheta by age six, Molumkin by age ten. He was fluent in six other native dialects before he learned English. At sixteen, he was inducted into the Quemcheta jaguar society, thus sealing our eventual claim to large tracts of land originally owned by that tribe. His Quemcheta connection gave him entree to primitive cultures denied most other white men, and it held him in good stead as far as his chosen field of anthropology. If anyone could have ferreted out secrets from the natives, it was my father."

"Bringing in an old friend, and that friend's friend, to profane sacred Indian ground?"

"A concern for common safety would have kept him from exploring alone, this far off the beaten path, among natives with a penchant for human flesh."

"So, where is this illusive cave complex?" Laura asked. It was another rhetorical question, but Jim tried an explanation anyway.

"Remember Wellernelling," he said, and those two words said a lot. "A vast cave network in north-central New Zealand? Estimated to include a two-hundred mile maze of interconnecting tunnels and passageways. Its subterranean caverns and galleries some of the biggest and most impressive in the world. Undiscovered for years. Why? Because its only link to the surface is a mile-long bolt hole so narrow and unobtrusive that it took a skinny, ten-year-old runaway to find and squeeze through. Proving bigness below ground doesn't necessarily advertise with a showy display at ground level. Meaning, if for twenty-four years this jungle hid our fathers' final campsite, how long can it hide a small hole?"

From necessity, Laura changed the subject: "Excuse me, but I need a minute in the powder room," she said and pushed herself to her feet.

Luckily, she didn't have to go far for privacy. She never did in a jungle so anxious and ever-ready to swallow anything and anybody. Nonetheless, she was always amazed by how quickly the I'm-the-only-person-left-alive illusion materialized whenever she took the few short steps necessary to separate her from pathway or campsite.

She was tucking in her blouse, no less encouraged by her state of affairs, when she saw someone. Her heart skipped a beat and her automatic response caught in her throat.

She'd only had a quick view, out of the corner of one eye, but it had been enough. If interrogated, she might never give a comprehensive description of the man, because he'd been too fast: she had no idea how tall he was or how much he weighed. Only her sixth sense told her she didn't know him from anytime before.

Light-headedly, she moved slowly, and not toward Jim and the campsite, but nearer the spot where the stranger had entered and exited her field of peripheral vision. She wanted to find evidence of his clandestine passing. She wanted verification she wasn't seeing things in some kind of waking nightmare.

She would never watch another horror film and ridicule characters who seemingly defied all logic by investigating alone.

They weren't illogical at all, as Laura now saw it. They merely needed to prove to themselves that the mind was a trickster, common sense bound to prevail when confronting nonexistent bogeymen head-on.

She stopped dead still. The hair on her arms began to rise, and her skin crawled, then solidified into pimply goose bumps. No part of her body escaped the accompanying chill.

Someone *was* there. Had sneaked up behind her. All Laura had to do was turn her head slowly to confront him. So, why not turn toward him? Why not confirm she was scared speechless by something more than a mere tree twisted by the elements into gargoyle form, or by something more than a mere shadow soon to be depleted of its pseudo malice by a shifting sun?

"Laura!"

She mustered all of her courage and turned, facing not a man but an animal. It was seven feet of disproportionately large head, compact body, sinuous muscle, and massive limbs, all stylishly wrapped in warm gold and cold black spots. Laura felt like a helpless fawn caught unawares, not a chance of escape or rescue.

"Laura!"

Its eyes were deepest darkness that locked hers and reflected absolutely nothing. They were windows on a savage world wherein horrible death and mutilation reigned supreme. They beckoned Laura to share the violence and become one with the jungle by sharing her lifeblood with it.

The beast could have her. It knew that. Laura knew that. In a brief moment of undeniable horror, Laura thought it wanted her more than it had ever wanted anyone or anything.

When the animal moved, it did so with unbelievable speed; there one minute, gone the next. It left only a quickly fading image in its wake.

"Do you believe that?" someone muttered, and Laura turned to find Jim, Joe, and Kurt standing there, all with drawn guns.

Her relief in seeing Kurt, combined with her relief in escaping the salivating jaws of the jungle cat, left her noticeably faint. She wiped her hand across her eyes to clear them of a sudden fogginess. Her legs would have given way completely if Kurt hadn't intuitively holstered his weapon and moved in to give her needed support. She clung to him in confirmation that he was real and not illusion.

"You're safe!" he assured her and pulled her close.

"*You're* safe!" she exclaimed, as much in response to seeing him saved from Jean-Michael's unknown fate as from the danger so recently offered them all by the jaguar. Her whole body pressed tighter to his for additional assurance that she wasn't dreaming.

All of the anger, pent up inside of her since Kurt had gone off with Joe against her express wishes, dissolved in her relief at seeing him alive.

"A jaguar," Jim superfluously identified. "Or, we could call it one of Captain Fortuna-Mata's 'exceptions,' if you'd prefer."

"One mighty *big* exception," Kurt observed, his voice slightly breathless from Laura's close call. "One apparently *not* scared away by the recent increase of foot traffic in the area. Makes me wonder how many other such impressive exceptions are awaiting down the trail."

Laura wasn't sure if she'd been rescued from the jaguar, or if the giant cat had regarded her as unsatisfactory eating. "I'm fine," she insisted and pushed Kurt away in a half-hearted manner that she hoped let him know she wasn't totally unappreciative.

"Sure?" he asked and, once again, tried to decide if her motives in breaking their physical contact were other than of a woman who preferred standing on her own.

"Yes, quite sure, thank you." More aware of his touch now that they were separated than when he'd held her. "And Jean-Michael?"

Kurt's expression in reply wasn't encouraging. Neither was his: "Not a trace. When we did hear something and followed it to its source, it turned out to be the jaguar."

"Well, *I* saw someone!" Laura insisted, her scrambled emotions back in check. "He didn't have four legs, either, even if he was creeping around in the underbrush."

"You saw someone? When?" Jim asked in rapid-fire succession.

"A few minutes before the jaguar showed," Laura said, "This time I'm sure it was a man, too."

"Not Jean-Michael?" Jim asked, although the answer was so obvious that Laura didn't bother answering.

"Any idea who, then?" Kurt injected, and he marveled at how his arms felt strangely empty without Laura filling them. When he'd hugged other women, under far more romantic conditions, had their aura lingered as long, once they'd stepped free? He tried hard to remember.

"I haven't a notion who he was," Laura admitted, "but, then, I have a limited selection of available men from which to choose: you, Jim, Joe, Jean-Michael, the captain."

"I don't understand what he'd be up to," Jim pondered aloud. "He could have done far more harm to us by now if he'd wanted. We're all babes in the woods, with the possible exception of Joe here."

"I think it's time we called someone in to help us answer just that kind of question," Laura insisted.

"As much as I was once reluctant to agree, I think Laura's right, this time, Jim," Kurt said. "She's definitely spotted some guy wandering around out there and that puts a whole new light on a lot of things, including Jean-Michael's disappearance. This stranger is no one we can any longer shuffle off to one side as a figment of overwrought imagination. Something strange is going on here. So strange we may very well need help."

"Granted, I don't like the idea of this mystery man and his possible connection to Jean-Michael's disappearance, but I remain reluctant to get the captain involved, only to discover there's a logical explanation for all of this," Jim said.

Laura prepared to argue that she didn't see any logical explanations.

"However," he added, "in this case, I think you both may be right. Let's radio the captain."

Laura breathed an audible sigh of relief. An unanimous decision was much better for the morale of all involved.

Jim led the way, then Joe, Laura, and Kurt brought up the rear. Kurt, like a mother hen, stuck close to Laura to prevent any need for a second miracle. His obvious protectiveness made Laura warm inside, and she flashed him a thank you smile just before the crowding underbrush forced him to step more completely behind her.

Jim stopped abruptly. Laura plowed into Joe, Kurt into her. She would have found humor in the chain reaction, but Joe's raised arm and Jim's audible hiss were too sobering for levity. Laura marveled as to how so much of her time in this stifling greenhouse environment was spent with goose bumps pimpling her flesh.

"What?" Kurt whispered, and his hand was on Laura's shoulder in welcome assurance that he was there. Without really thinking, Laura raised her hand to cover his and gave a squeeze of thanks. Only when she was more acutely aware of his hand's strong presence beneath her fingers did she consciously allow her hand to slip free.

'Maybe nothing," Jim admitted, and his voice sounded normal. "I thought I left my backpack propped against that stump."

Kurt reluctantly removed his hand from Laura's shoulder. Then Joe, Laura, and he followed Jim into the small break in the forest that held their campsite.

If Jim was reassured, Laura wasn't. When she'd left him, she knew Jim's backback *had* been against the stump, not laid beside it. He hadn't moved it when he'd gotten the Granola bar he'd eaten during their talk, either. If he didn't remember moving it, after that, who was to say that he had? "The radio!" Laura warned, her voice strained by the dawning of those possible implications.

They rushed in unison, Jim the first to reach his gear and retrieve a small, space-age marvel enclosed by light-weight plastic.

Their mutual laughter was the result of nervous embarrassment, like members of a horror-movie audience who'd been suckered into a scare by nothing at all.

Laura was reassured by the static immediately forthcoming from the radio. It took her longer to realize Jim and Kurt weren't as pleased by the erratic sound effects.

"This is Kenner-Reiger-Lexly calling Captain Fortuna-Mata," Jim said. "Come in."

Jim and Kurt frowned. "What's wrong?" Laura asked. Jim's repeat of the call, and the continued static, increased Laura's sense of unease.

"I don't think the radio is working," Kurt said, his explanation, by then, superfluous. Laura knew it wasn't working, as surely as she knew it hadn't malfunctioned on its own.

Jim apparently wasn't prepared to take Laura's quite-so-dramatic stand: "It could have been jarred on the ride in," he rationalized. "I wasn't as careful as I might have been, more tired and careless than I care to admit."

"A radio like this is designed to be jarred, isn't it!" Laura said. She didn't know anything about what made a radio work, but she knew they must be built to withstand far more than was delivered to this one. It was one more thing that didn't ring true.

"Let me take a look at it," Kurt requested. Among his other business-oriented positions, he was the president of a Reiger company that manufactured computer chips.

Jim handed it over, and Kurt used the screwdriver of his Swiss Army knife to detach a panel of red plastic. He uncovered a part of the interior that was a maze of tiny components.

"Here's the problem," he said. His forefinger pointed; Laura found the spot no more disordered than the rest. "Unfortunately, it's not something we're going to put right with what we have available."

"The result of jarring?" Laura asked. She didn't sound hysterical, but it took a good deal of conscious effort not to.

Kurt shrugged. "That's certainly a possibility. Considering our alternatives, it's a pretty good one."

"Well, I have an alternative just as likely," Laura put forward. "I say someone was here while we were entertaining that jaguar. Whatever is broken is broken because someone purposely broke it." Her voice had risen a good octave. She found it difficult to breathe through throat muscles gone tight with tension. She willed herself to relax.

Jim and Kurt looked at each other and at her as if her notion was somehow unique; but, surely, she wasn't the only one who saw events as more than purely coincidental.

"Why didn't this mysterious someone just take the radio?" Jim pressed, and Laura thought he sounded patronizing. "Why go to the bother of screwing up a few circuits or whatever?"

"Because, for whatever his reasons, he doesn't want us pointing an accusing finger in his direction," Laura said. "If he took the radio, we'd know he was out there. This way, we blame you for jarring it on the trip in."

That brought a round of silence, interrupted by Kurt: "A cat playing with four mice?" Laura didn't find the thought a pleasant one.

"Either of you have any enemy harboring an old grudge?" Jim asked.

"I refused a bank loan to Fieldback Florists," Laura volunteered in a weak attempt at humor. "They, however, would have needed to float a loan elsewhere to come up with the cash for a hit-man."

"If someone wanted to harm one of us, or all of us, he would have had plenty of opportunity," Kurt reminded. "Especially if that someone were skilled enough to dispose of Jean-Michael without a hitch."

"We don't know he disposed of Jean-Michael," Jim argued.

"You think Jean-Michael chose that particular moment to go AWOL?" Laura asked, flabbergasted by Jim's reluctance to face facts.

"Stranger things have happened," Jim observed too authoritatively for Laura's taste.

"Well, I don't believe it!" Laura disagreed. She didn't know much about Jean-Michael's lot in the Brazilian army, but her intuition had held her in pretty good stead until now.

"Maybe our mysterious stranger isn't ready yet to make his move," Kurt suggested. "Whatever that move may be. Could he have eliminated Jean-Michael because Jean-Michael forced his hand by coming after him?"

"Maybe he has a reason of his own for wanting us to go on," Laura conjectured along those same lines. "Maybe he's playing his cards so as not to spook us."

"You're insinuating we're not spooked?" Jim asked disbelievingly.

Laura suspected he'd been magnanimous with his "we're,"

really meaning Laura was already spooked. Well, he was right! "Spooked or not, we *are* going on, aren't we?" she challenged. Let him disagree with that if he could. They were in good physical shape and only a short distance from where they wanted to be. The only verifiable thing that had threatened them was a jaguar, not a man. She didn't need any count of votes to know the final tally was still stacked in favor of continuance.

Hiking out for help was no real solution in that it would take four days to get out, another four days to get back in, plus additional time for searching: odds against Jean-Michael, by anyone's count. It would take just as long to seek assistance from the botanists at the deNali caves. But they owed Jean-Michael one last-ditch effort to find him before they continued on, so they nervously risked lack of visual contact with one another and settled for calling back and forth as they combed the underbrush.

Laura was more exhausted by the searching than by any regular day of jungle trekking. A normal day meant they picked and chose the route of least resistance, usually one of the animal runs crisscrossing most stretches of jungle. A search, though, required a purposeful examination of even the most densely vegetated and hard-to-reach places.

Of minor consolation, Laura feared the mystery man far less now that she'd seen him.

"Anything?" Kurt greeted through a break in the foliage, and it was the first time Laura had seen him in over an hour.

"Nothing," she admitted, frustrated and disappointed. "Absolute zilch."

She combed a hand through her short hair, and her fingers caught in the tangles. A shower of twigs and leaf fragments was dislodged. Laura didn't even want to think what living things her fingers had left undisturbed.

More of the same, until nightfall, didn't leave anyone a bundle of energy or good cheer. By mutual consent, they didn't cook but ate high-calorie trail bars instead.

Though Laura thought she was too tired to sleep, she was wrong.

When her dream came, it was of the sort that she could say, even in dreaming: "This isn't happening!" However, the subconscious saying didn't make it less real or unsettling.

In it, she tried to fight her way through clinging undergrowth. She thrashed about and made no progress whatsoever. Vines wrapped her arms and hands. Roots wrapped her feet and legs. Lianas trailed her body like Medusa-hair.

The jungle was eating her alive, as it had devoured Jean-Michael, and as it had swallowed Jim's father, Kurt's father, and her father.

In front of her, vegetation parted like curtains on a stage. She saw Jean-Michael on the ground. The jagged edges of a broken bone protruded through the flesh of his leg.

Laura called, but he didn't answer. He didn't even look. So, she called for Jim and Kurt who were somewhere near but unseen. They didn't come or respond, either.

What did come was a man sheathed in shadow. Laura knew he was up to no good. She sensed his evil eyes and his malicious sneer. She sensed his deadly gun.

"No!" she screamed, but she made no sound.

His gun, though, made noise enough to wake her.

She was drenched in sweat and breathed erratically. It took seemingly forever to realize where she was.

"Thunder," Kurt whispered, his hammock hung close to hers. "There's a storm somewhere." In proof, the thunder rumbled again.

"My nightmare wake you?" Laura asked, worried it might have. Kurt needed his sleep as much as she needed hers.

"My own bugbears keep me awake," he absolved.

Laura suspected his nightly phantoms revolved more around where this little group was going than around where they were now or had been. She wanted to reassure him and, against her better judgment, extended her hand beyond her mosquito netting to find his fingers.

"We'll be there soon," she said and gave his hand a reassuring squeeze.

"And we'll only arrive twenty-four years too late," Kurt commented bitterly under his breath.

More thunder roared in the distance. As for the sky directly overhead, neither Kurt nor Laura could tell if it was cloud-covered or star-filled. The ever-present barrier of limbs and leaves shrouded their view.

"If anyone can put together the pieces, we can," Jim joined in. Apparently, sleep had escaped him, too, despite the exhaustion of the day. "Certain people become sensitized by reacting with each other, with places, with things. My gut-feeling says there are clues to our fathers' fate to be found here that only the three of us can find."

"Yes," Laura agreed.

"Maybe," Kurt qualified, not prepared to be as certain about their combined psychic powers as Jim and Laura seemed to be.

"Let's get some sleep," Jim suggested. "Too many more days like today, and we won't be fit to succeed at what brings us here."

"Sleeping is easier said than done," Laura observed, dropping Kurt's hand and attempting to get comfortable in the hammock. Except, somewhere down the line, minutes or hours later, the thunder even more distant, she did sleep. Her dreams were blessedly unremembered in the morning, but they left a bizarre aftertaste.

Over a breakfast that consisted of trail bars washed down with warm water, they discussed Jean-Michael's fate. "We've done all we can," Jim said. "If we haven't found any trace of him by now, it's doubtful we'll ever turn up anything."

"Agreed. But Joe should be sent back to the runway to bring in a search party," Kurt said. "Jean-Michael deserves all the odds we can stack in his favor."

With a weary heart, Laura watched Joe's retreat into the jungle. Then, with weary mind and body, she headed off in the opposite direction with Jim and Kurt. Beneath her feet, leaf-bloated loam rebounded like springy moss; and, whatever wounds had been inflicted upon nature yesterday, by less than ecology-conscious searchers who had plowed through the underbrush, they seemed miraculously healed during the night. "What little difference we make to all of this," Laura said, the thought anything but comforting.

Laura shrugged her shoulders to adjust the ride of her pack on her back, and, the weight aligned in a balance almost comfortable, she stoically headed on her way.

"Will we ever know what happened to Jean-Michael?" Laura asked at their first rest break. She was seated by a small waterfall that tumbled over moss-green rocks into a nearby pool. Rare sunlight bathed lavender orchids perched precariously on a dead log at the water's edge. Waxy green leaves, like exotic life forms, drooped to the mirror surface as if to drink. In another time frame, Laura might have found it beautiful. Now, she saw only a facade behind which lurked the truly ugly reality.

"Maybe someday we'll know what happend to him," Kurt said optimistically and tossed a stone into the water. The water exuded spirals of green sediment from the bottom of the pool.

The swirls were more reminders of just how easily the outwardly attractive veneer could be stripped away.

"In another twenty-four years, we may know, you mean?" Laura asked cynically. She took a good look at Kurt and knew what he was going to say. "If then," she said right along with him.

They smiled at their shared talent for second-guessing.

When they headed off again, each and every step convinced Laura she moved further and further from any chance of solving Jean-Michael's disappearance. Her same steps, however, brought her closer to discovering the answer to an even longer-lasting mystery. Very near where she now walked, she knew three men, one very near and dear to her, another once like a second father, had dropped out of sight, their disappearance a legacy still haunting the lives of the people left behind.

At noon, Laura didn't want to stop. She was that anxious for the ultimate distraction of tracking down on-the-spot clues.

"It won't do any of us any good to arrive weak and undernourished," Jim argued.

Still begrudging the delay, Laura removed her pack.

"I need fresh air," she said between bites of carob and raisins. She found it hard to believe that, up there above her, somewhere, was enough air in flux to make helicopter flying dangerous, when at ground level there wasn't even the vaguest hint of a breeze. She nodded toward a steep pathway rain-carved in a nearby upthrust of rock, her air-starved lungs demanding she disregard her intuition that it was better to stay together. "Give me a call when you're ready to pull out," she instructed.

"I'll come with you," Kurt volunteered, and Laura didn't object, although she somehow thought she might be better off if she did. There was something disconcerting about the idea of Kurt and her alone.

"If nobody minds, I'll stay put," Jim said. He crouched comfortably with his back against a tree and settled in.

"Maybe we shouldn't split up?" Laura suggested.

"Nonsense!" Jim protested, and Laura couldn't tell if he were as tired as he insinuated, or if he thought he was doing Kurt and her some kind of favor, by giving them some time to themselves. Laura suspected the latter, and his continued streak of misplaced romanticism piqued her no end. "You will hear a caterwauling you won't believe, come the very first sign of trouble," Jim promised. "It's not as if you're going far. You'll be lucky if the few steps you manage up that rock pile even penetrate the treetops. Even if they do, there's no guarantee you'll get through to fresh air."

As it turned out, the steep path looped around the rock to where treetops immediately obliged by opening. Laura led Kurt up above the trees as far as the full blaze of the tropical sun, but she paused momentarily before a final, sizable step in the rock; during which time, Kurt moved past her and up with consummate skill. He turned back from his achieved summit and automatically offered her his hand in assistance.

Laura hesitated, then grabbed it, pulling herself on up the rocks. She sat down on a stone slab that overlooked the carpeting of green-clogged landscape. Dense clouds covered the tips of several rocky spires along the horizon and hinted of the thunder that had punctuated the night before. Dark slash marks in the sky denoted a deluge in progress.

Ironically, Laura found air above tree-level even hotter than within the "belly of the monster." Nevertheless, there was the accompanying lift to her spirits in having escaped, even for the moment, the claustrophobia rampant among the trees.

"Sit here!" she braved by patting a spot directly next to her on the hard stone.

Kurt made no move to join her.

"How about if I promise not to bite?" Laura said. She patted the spot again, determined that he not refuse her. She had things to say that would hopefully put their relationship in better perspective.

"I'll stand," he rebelled and leaned against a stone buttress for support. He didn't want to sit next to her, because he wanted so much to sit there; if that were contradictory, he refused to analyze it any further.

Laura accepted his decision to keep his distance. In the end, she was even thankful for it. She needed a clear head, and there was something about Kurt that made his nearness conducive to light-headedness. For a long while, she'd successfully attributed all such disconcerting cause and effect to the place, to the heat, to the humidity, to the circumstances. Now, she knew differently, no matter how long she'd been able to delude herself into rejecting the reality. There was simply something about this man, from among all the men she'd ever met or known, which could make her downright giddy whenever he gave her a mere glance or a passing touch. Therefore, it was past time to accept the reality and lock all the shutters in the face of the horrendous potential of any building emotional storm.

"Do you remember my mad schoolgirl crush on you when I was a kid?" she asked and watched his expression. Anyway, she tried to watch it. The hurt way he looked down at the ground, rather than at her, made reading his face difficult if not impossible.

"No, I don't remember," he said finally, and he still didn't look up.

"I didn't remember, either," Laura surprised, and he looked up to read her expression and see what she was up to; her appealing good looks made him self-consciously return his gaze to the ground. "But, shall I tell you who *did* remember?" she asked, then didn't wait for his answer, because she wanted to make sure he didn't head her off at the pass with either real or feigned disinterest. "My mother remembered."

"Your mother?" he queried and looked up. The mere mention of June Lexly seemed incantation enough to summon up the enemy, and he folded his arms across his powerful chest in a readily identifiable defensive posture.

"Mother didn't want me to come, you know?" Laura said. "She used all sorts of arguments to keep me from it. Didn't pull any punches, either. One of which was to ask me if I really wanted to dredge up childhood love fantasies and subject them to the perils of my more mature spinster's longings." She smiled, despite the pain she'd felt at the time and felt now in remembering.

"That's how my old-fashioned mother sees me," she continued. "As a spinster who never got herself a man and somehow feels less the woman because of it. Someone so disappointed in the blow of being left single that I'm willing to make one last-ditch effort: grab for the rekindling of a childhood infatuation with the man whose father had not only possibly killed my father but had plunged my mother into a bitter pit from which she's never managed to crawl free."

"I do sometimes forget I'm not the only one whose life was turned upside down," he said, genuinely sorry how June's life, as well as his and Laura's, had been so affected by something over which none of them had had any control.

Laura savored a rare breath of fresh air that somehow had managed to survive the journey through the miles of sucking heat that existed between her and distant rain clouds. The coolness was short-lived and made the return to normality even more oppressive.

"Mother's misconceptions, of course, are the bane of her generation," she diagnosed. "She grew up in a world where a woman-content-with-a-career was still pretty much an anomaly, where any woman was still pretty much incomplete without a man. So, I forgave her her insinuations that I was less than content with my life and my career, when I was so obviously pleased with both. As for her references to my supposed desire to resurrect some long-dead childhood puppy love, I'm afraid I was far less kind. In point of fact, I told her she was frankly crazy; at age eleven, my feelings for you, as I recalled them, were certainly more those of a younger sister for her brother than of a Juliet for her Romeo."

She gave a breathless sigh and might have left it all at that, but she was determined to proceed now that she had the ball rolling. How many times had she laid aside a book she was reading, or frowned at some TV or theatrical production, when she realized there'd be no complications of plot if ever the characters just sat down for a very few minutes and just got everything out in the open? She was determined that her life wasn't going to proceed helter-skelter, like some soap opera, for lack of communication.

"As it turns out, it seems I owe my mother a partial apology," she continued and found a handkerchief in her blouse pocket with which to wipe away the sweat beading on her upper lip and forehead.

"Oh?" Kurt asked and looked up. She definitely had his attention.

"Because the minute you stepped out of the plane at Septiaola, took my hand, and spoke my name, I knew that, yes, the boy-inside-the-man was someone on whom I'd had a crush, right up until the time you disappeared from my life. I'd just somehow managed to erase those feelings when confronted, at the time, with all the accusations leveled against your father; and you not around to defend him."

"We went to Colorado," Kurt could now explain, years after the fact. "One of dad's companies had a place at Aspen, and mother thought it would get us away from the reporters, not to mention away from your mother. As it turned out, of course, the news media followed, though your mother kept away. My mother, you know, went to her grave never really able to understand why June was so easily convinced of my father's guilt."

"Jealousy, pure and simple," Laura explained, because that motivation was one her mother had long ago been helped to accept. "Although, maybe not so simple. She resented, you see, the way dad and I were seduced by your father's interest in spelunking. She never could figure out what all the fuss was about in squirreling around underground, and, suddenly, my father was regularly packing his things in order to spend long periods of time doing just that with Karl, rather than being content to stay at home with her. Then, when dad disappeared while on just such a spelunking expedition— *with Karl*—well, something inside her snapped. As neither Karl nor dad was around to blame, mom leveled all her pent-up frustrations at you and your mother. Nor, am I afraid, has all the counseling, or the conference talks by the General Authorities about the healing benefits of forgiveness, wrought any miracle cures. Thus, her ability to misconstrue why I found this expedition so important."

Kurt wondered where this conversation would take them.

"Remember in the tent the night before we were to head out?" she asked; he wasn't apt to forget it. "My telling you how I wanted to know for certain my father is dead: that remains the most important thing in my life. Uncertainty doesn't allow a cessation of mourning. I'd like to bracket that trauma of my life, once and for all, and not leave it so open-ended."

"You're not here, then, to renew that childhood crush on me?" Kurt asked, deciding there was a need for a bit of levity in the proceedings.

"Schoolgirl infatuations, by definition, are nothing else," Laura said and returned his smile. "I'm no longer a schoolgirl, nor have I been for a long time. If circumstances hadn't forced me to dissolve the crush I had on you, the normal course of growing older would have done the deed."

"Oh," Kurt replied with more disappointment than he cared to admit.

"As if you really even noticed — at the time," Laura said. "I really must have been pretty pathetic, mooning around over someone four years my senior."

"I always remember you as pretty, never pathetic," he complimented and wondered if she knew how he'd enshrined that time-before-the-tragedy, her included within it, as the happiest time of his life. No, he didn't think she knew, and, until he was more sure of the course of their conversation, he wouldn't tell her, either. He was suspicious that Laura-the-girl, whom he'd relegated to his "dream-time," might already have colored the way he responded to Laura-the-woman.

"That doesn't mean I wasn't tempted by the idea of seeing you again, after all of these years," Laura said. "Mother got that part right, even if she did distort it beyond redemption. I have a like curiosity, too, about other people who entered my life briefly and then faded away."

"Curiosity to see the son of the man who may have killed your father?"

"Curiosity to see someone who was once a good friend and companion," Laura corrected. "Do believe me when I say that I've read all the newspaper accounts about the disappearances of our fathers, and, unlike my mother, I've evolved no clear conviction of your father's guilt, or his innocence."

If she didn't hate him, because he was his father's son, she made Kurt wonder at the explanation behind her skittishness every time he'd touched her.

"You wonder why I shy away from you on occasion?" Laura divined: such an incident the catalyst for this talk in the first place.

"I wonder that, yes," Kurt confessed, convinced she'd read his mind.

It's not because I'm repulsed," she assured and dabbed her mouth, her cheeks, and her forehead with her handkerchief. "Nor is it because I doubt that, whenever you offer me a hand, you do so solely as a genuine Good Samaritan, without ulterior motive. Nonetheless, each time it happens, and this is because of an admittedly personal quirk of my own, I 'think' I find myself interpreting more than you intend, more than there is. I qualify that with an 'I think,' because I'm not fully sure what I *do* feel at such times. I do know for sure, though, and have known from the start, that I don't particularly want to examine those feelings any closer."

She could tell that left him confused. Frankly, it left her embarrassed, and she was surprised she had confessed so much of what, until now, she'd denied even to herself.

"I don't quite understand," he said on cue.

"Let me put it this way," Laura tried to spell out what she thought she might finally have grasped herself. "You're someone from a happy time in my life, someone I've finally managed successfully to disassociate from whatever horrors your father may or may not have committed. I liked you once, I like you now. If it were only you and I in this equation, it would be different. Unfortunately . . ."

"There's your mother," he finished for her and couldn't help wonder if all of her talk about her indefinable "feelings" toward him weren't just rationalizations to cover the real reasons—the same as her mother's—for her repulsion.

"Yes," she agreed, "there is my mother. She loved my father. She loves me. If I regret that she's been less than objective in all of this, that doesn't make me love her any the less. I've hurt her in going against her wishes to come this far, and I think about that hurt quite often. I'm not prepared, nor willing, to do anything else to make her life more miserable than it already is. I hope you understand and realize that my standoffishness, therefore, isn't a reflection on you but has to do entirely with me and certain idiosyncratic feelings I'd just as soon not explore further for fear of whatever potential complications they could add to my life. Does any of that make sense?" She frowned. "It does seem to have come out a bit jumbled."

"And if we find the remains of three people out here?" Kurt queried and knew she'd have far more reason to be concerned if she knew of his inner, almost uncontrollable, impulses which compelled him to touch her and to be near her since the first moment of their reunion. "My father's remains included."

"Confirm, you mean, that he didn't engineer the disappearances as a cover in making his escape to one of the other South American countries to avoid apprehension and prosecution for war crimes against humanity?"

"Your mother would be hard-pressed to continue her vendetta in the face of that new evidence, wouldn't she?"

"Wellernelling," Laura threw out: the same argument Jim had used when the two were discussing the odds in favor of their coming up with something when all others had failed.

"New Zealand, mile-long bolt hole, runaway boy, massive cave complex below ground, undiscovered for years."

"This jungle could hide indefinitely a similarly small and insignificant access to its caves," she reminded and wondered if she really did wish she could lower her guard, just a bit, to explore the potential of their renewed relationship. No matter, though, that misguided thinking? She had to deal with reality, and now that her fears were all out, all on the table, she hoped Kurt would help her proceed without unnecessary complications added to those already encountered as a result of Jean-Michael's disappearance, not to mention the complications Laura figured were still ahead. Why shouldn't he? Never, for a moment, did she believe their touching made *his* insides turn cartwheels. He was probably as anxious to nip any silliness in the bud as she was.

"Hey, you two!" Jim called from somewhere below. "I'm on my last mouthful of health biscuit."

"Heading down!" Laura assured, thankful for her exit line and ready to leave on it.

"Yes," Kurt agreed and pushed himself away from the stone buttress in order to precede her down the pathway. Obviously, she had her life in order, even if his life was in no way as neatly catalogued.

Laura couldn't shake a sudden masochistic feeling that she had somehow just cut off her nose to spite her face. Such a feeling made her uneasy as she watched Kurt's back muscles moving beneath his shirt as he retreated before her. Helplessly, her gaze traveled the length of his compact body, from his strong back, to his sinewy legs, to his feet encased within their scuffed hiking boots.

Unexpectedly, she was distracted, at that point, by the tip of something pressed into a small cushion of dirt by the passing pressure of Kurt's heel. She bent for a closer look, and a tingling exhilaration sunburst through her as she confirmed what she already suspected.

"Laura?" Kurt asked. Although he'd had his back toward her, he'd known the moment she'd stopped following. He turned to face her and found her kneeling on the ground. "Laura?" he asked again, genuinely concerned.

She heard him, but she didn't immediately answer him, too busy in her survey of the rocks above and around her. Excitedly, she sought the illusive origin of the prize she had rescued from the dust and now held cupped securely in her right hand.

4

As easily as had Kurt and Laura, Jim recognized the significance of Laura's find. "Great!" he congratulated. "Absolutely fantastic." He held the seashell between his forefinger and thumb for a closer look. "Definitely gastropod. Definitely fossilized. No modern-day Indian carted this shell from the sea for barter or for eating its contents, did he? It swam in an ocean that existed right here, where there's now only jungle. It died here and sank here, with others of its kind, to compress eventually into layer upon layer of soft limestone."

"We've come up with a breakthrough that has escaped every so-called expert who ever said this area is too completely capped by hard igneous lava flows to have any soft sedimentary rock anywhere near the surface! This says there's at least one spot where sedimentary deposits, easily carved by the elements, are accessible from ground level." Laura paused.

"Where the wind and the water could have hollowed out tunnels and galleries. Where three men could have disappeared. Where we can follow. Great good show, Laura!" Jim said and placed his free hand on her forearm and gave a congratulatory squeeze in emphasis. Laura automatically compared the nonelectric results to those more memorable sensations she invariably experienced in the wake of Kurt's touch.

"Unfortunately, what's left of the limestone deposit that contained that fossil isn't much," Laura reluctantly admitted but didn't add how disappointed that admission made her.

"Most of the great cave complexes of the world have been sculptured by water in just the kind of soft rock this seashell has been a part of all these years, hasn't it?" Jim continued excitedly, as if refusing to be put off by even a hint of pessimism. "Oh, there are caves in harder rock, even in volcanic rock when a sluggish crust formed around a tongue of lava that kept on flowing to leave a hollow tube behind, but we know how comparatively small those are, don't we?"

Laura led him the rest of the way up into the rocks to where Kurt waited. She expected a decided loss of his optimism as soon as he saw what they really had.

"Well, Laura has done all right by us, hasn't she, Jim?" Kurt greeted. He stood by the pitiful example of weathered-to-gray stone from which he'd plucked several more fossilized seashells. He wasn't disappointed, and he didn't sound or look disappointed, any more than Jim did.

Laura basked in his compliment but couldn't help feel her find was destined to disillusion all of them. They needed more than this small pocket of sedimentary limestone at the tip of this isolated pile of rock. "No caves here," she pointed out superfluously.

"We needn't expect all our clues to be easily deciphered," Jim chided gently. He examined the several new fossils Kurt had recovered. Then, he ran his hand along the exposed surface of weathered stone. Pieces of deteriorating rock and shell came loose like large flakes of dandruff. "If this is less than we might have hoped for, let's not get discouraged until we've analyzed it more carefully."

His fingers traced the parallel striations as visible in the stone as lines were visible on a piece of notebook paper.

"Sediments," he identified, obviously as much to refresh his own memory as theirs, "formed like thin sheets piled to great heights on a level ocean bed. Since this particular bit of one stack is tilted, no longer flat as it was originally, let's assume some force of nature buckled up a mountain out of that long-ago ocean bed, and the ocean drained away."

"You want us to imagine how it was after that initial buckling tilted the sedimentary layers off their horizontal plane?" Kurt asked intuitively.

"Exactly!" Jim agreed, like a teacher bestowing an "A" to a particularly astute student. "Better yet, pretend we're here when the actual buckling occurs to leave us suddenly lifted high and dry somewhere on the side of that mountain. Even as we watch, year after year of erosion begins. Rain carves out the soft mountain with deep gullies and with wide valleys. Wind gouges out Swiss-cheese designs in the yielding stone. Suddenly, the mountain doesn't look like a mountain any more but like isolated pinnacles, much like this one here. Then, a nearby volcano erupts and fills up with molten lava all of the cavities and grooves in the landscape. What the magma misses, though, are those pinnacles of sedimentary stone that are the last pieces of the mountain. The pinnacles survive like islands in a stream, only to wear away years later into sinkholes that give rain and water access to all that other soft stone trapped beneath the lava on every side."

"What we need to know, then, is where some of those islands of sedimentary stone survived and eroded away amid the lava flows," Kurt said.

"The top of the original mountain is long gone," Laura joined in. Class participation had been her forte in college. She hadn't done badly in geology, either. She readily saw how the upper edge of these tilted layers ended abruptly.

"And the bottom of the mountain?" Jim challenged.

Laura's gaze followed the downward direction of the same tilted layers. When the rock ended all too quickly, Laura's gaze continued as if parts of the mountain, long gone, still existed. She ended up looking at a depression of jungle not all that far away as the crow flies. "There could be some of this sedimentary rock down there," she said and pointed. "Some of it covered by lava, but possibly some not. Over the years water may have percolated to hollow out larger sections of the softer rock trapped beneath the blanket of lava."

"It will, of course, depend upon a lot of things having gone just right," Jim said. "If all of the mountain, but this one piece upon which we stand, eroded before the lava covered it all, there'll be nothing down there but the thin layer of topsoil and the thicker layers of hard rock so typical of this area. It's only if there were those other remnants of the mountain, able to survive the lava, like islands in a stream, eroding later into sinkholes, that we hit the jackpot."

"I say we take a closer look," Kurt proposed.

"How far is 'down there' from our fathers' last campsite?" Laura asked.

"They might have made it on an overnight hike," Jim answered. "A light backpack is all they would have needed."

"Then, we should definitely check it out," Laura voted. Besides, she wanted her discovery of the fossilized seashell to be more important than she now saw it. She wanted sinkholes among those trees. She wanted Karl Reiger dead down there and not hiding out alive somewhere. She wanted vindication for Kurt. All of which made her heart beat faster, as she told herself not to expect too many miracles.

Getting where they'd decided to go was hard going. It confirmed Laura's contention that nothing about this environment was conducive to ease and comfortable living. She detected malicious intent in every root that tripped her, in every branch that scratched her, in every animal run that didn't head in the direction they were headed.

Every step seemed to mean blazing their own trail. Jim and Kurt wielded machetes like every explorer in every jungle movie Laura had ever seen.

She was hot, but she was used to being hot. She was drenched in sweat, but what else was new? She was bitten so often by bugs, seen and unseen, that their bite marks had formed a rash seemingly a permanent part of her flushed complexion. Scratching was becoming second nature.

She mentally isolated every rock she saw and classified it as sedimentary, igneous, or metamorphic. She prayed for soft sedimentary rock; she got hard igneous.

"Here!" Jim said and brought the group to a halt in a spot hardly different from a thousand more they'd seen that day and the days before.

Laura was disappointed and didn't want it to be the place. It gave no indications of what they wanted. Brigham Young's followers she thought, couldn't have been any more unimpressed by their first glimpse of the Great Salt Lake valley.

"What say we set up camp and, then, look around until nightfall?" Jim suggested.

Laura was torn between her anxiousness to explore and her suspicions of disappointment. Nonetheless, within fifteen minutes of starting to look, she discovered a long, narrow, and very deep split in the earth. She found it by almost stumbling into it. If she hadn't stopped to ponder the origin of distant water sounds, she would have mistaken the carpet-like weave of vines at her feet as backed by solid ground. When she realized she was poised on the brink of an abyss, she got so sick in the pit of her stomach, and so dizzy in the bargain, she barely managed to look up in time to warn Kurt: "Watch out!" she screamed. His possibly falling victim to the trap prompted an ache inside her more intense than any fear or dizziness spawned by her teetering on the brink. Luckily, like her, his reflexes were honed by previous exposure to the surprises the jungle had to offer.

Her scream brought Jim running, and Laura quickly explained: "I don't think there's a thing supporting any of those vines in front of us."

Kurt nudged the deceptive cover of vegetation with his foot. "I think you're right," he confirmed. "And do I hear water?" He cocked his head in just the way Jean-Michael had done upon hearing someone in the darkness.

Laura was overcome by a renewal of the paranoia which insisted she was still being watched. She would have suspected the hidden watcher of having dug the trench if it weren't so obviously nature-made.

Jim and Kurt, in the meantime, tore away some of the concealing vines.

"It's possibly what we're looking for, isn't it?" Kurt voiced excitedly.

"You think so?" Laura responded, refocusing her attention.

"Well, it's not the Grand Canyon," Jim said, on his knees at the edge of the narrow chasm, "but it's long and it's deep. I'd say, there's a good cross section of geological history on display down there."

"Yes," Laura agreed, and her excitement took precedence over everything else, and that included her paranoia.

They cleared more of the vines, and Laura spotted a couple places where she might have stepped over the crack and not even known it was there. Mainly, though, the fissure yawned from three to four feet wide, and that was plenty wide to swallow anyone.

As for how deep the crack went, Laura couldn't tell. Water, running along the bottom, was audible, but the narrowness of the fissure kept the depths in darkness.

"Well, Laura, do you want to go down for a closer look?" Jim asked and scrambled to his feet. "I can't argue your right to go first. Kurt?"

"I don't think I even thanked her from keeping me from checking it out before her — without a rope," Kurt said. He was a little embarrassed by his oversight. "Did I, Laura?"

"Either of you would have done the same for me," Laura said, and she didn't doubt it for a minute. Kurt alive was thank you enough.

"So, then," Jim said, "I'll get the equipment you'll need."

He disappeared into the trees, and Laura was acutely aware of how close Kurt stood to her. It struck her as somehow sad that two different people, left in a similar situation, might well have hugged and kissed in anticipatory excitement. Laura's talk with Kurt, though, hampered even the most spontaneous of intimacies. However, if she had taken care of the possibilities for any such physical contact between them, Laura could do little to offset the unbelievable way she still felt whenever he was near her.

Gratefully, Jim wasn't gone long, soon back with a "Ready?"

"Yes, I'm ready," she said.

"Okay," Jim anchored one end of the rope to a tree.

Laura knew how to rappel down a rope. It required her leaning backward from the edge of a cliff with the rope passed under one thigh, across her body, and over her opposite shoulder, and walking down the face at almost a right angle. It was one of the first skills she'd learned as an amateur spelunker. However, the narrowness of this particular crack, even at its widest, made a light-weight harness a better idea, and she fastened on the one Jim gave her. While she was at it, she donned a plastic hard hat with a miner's lamp and secured its strap tightly around her chin.

She didn't drop as quickly to the bottom as she might have. She controlled her slide for a gradual descent that enabled her to examine each and every layer of dirt and rock bared when the stream had cut through.

Nearest the top was a surprisingly shallow layer of topsoil from which roots of plants and trees protruded in a thick matting that hinted of subterranean battles waged for scarce nutrients. Topsoil quickly gave way to weathered lava which gave way to hard lava. Wedding-cake layers of hard, black igneous stripes followed. It was a record of one massive magma flow after another. The deeper Laura got, the more she was convinced there was nothing here for them. After long centuries, this stone showed little signs of disintegration, even here where one stream had labored for years to carve a narrow foothold.

The fissure widened at the bottom. Laura looked up and felt as if she were in a fat-bottomed bottle. Her perspective gave her a better idea of the extent of the crack. Dull light twinkled through the vine cover above and made a narrow ribbon of dim sparklers as far to the right as she could see. To the left, her view was blocked by a slight jog in the fissure's line of direction.

"Any luck?" Kurt asked and leaned over the edge; his head,

neck, and shoulders provided a dark silhouette.

"Nothing but basalt or the equivalent, and I'm touching bottom — now!" Laura informed and tried not to be disappointed. Her feet hit wet surface. "I'm unfastening for a better look." Her voice was made full-bodied by the unique accoustics. "The stream must have seen better days, because it's unlikely it did all of this carving at its present trickle. I'm standing midstream with no danger of waterlogged feet."

The water flowed from the right, and Laura followed it left around the small bend.

She stopped dead in her tracks, surprised that what she saw was what she wanted to see. The main streambed swept straight ahead, but, to the right, where sedimentary deposits once might or might not have offered their soft stone for carving, there was a cave entrance.

"Something!" Laura called, and her voice trembled with her excitement.

"Whereabouts are you?" Kurt called back.

By voice, they pinpointed her below them. Then, they ripped away another large section of vines. The removal did nothing toward alleviating the dimness at the bottom of the crack.

"Looks like a cave," Laura informed, her head thrown back as she looked up at them. Her heart was beating with excitement, and she experienced the headiness of adrenaline turned loose inside her.

"Hold tight, I'm coming down!" Kurt informed.

"You'll have more maneuverability if you make your descent a bit farther along," she instructed. "Through here, it's narrow most of the way down."

"Read you, loud and clear."

He ripped away more vines once Laura got him conveniently positioned. He threw his rope over the side; Laura stepped back out of the way. He didn't waste time with a harness but came down hand over hand. Laura, her eyes finally adjusted to the absence of light, watched the ease with which he came. Once again, she wondered how it might have been different for them if. . . . She consciously rejected any such daydreams and concentrated on how her standing where she was was reminiscent of holding a giant shell to her ear and listening to the dull roar of the sea trapped inside. Except, on second thought, she found it strange how the sound didn't really seem to be coming from the hollow cave at all.

Kurt touched bottom. "Thunder?" he asked.

Laura experienced disquieting déjà vu and tried to define it.

Stones came loose from the layer of root matting and topsoil above her, and they soon made metallic sounds as they deflected off Laura's hard hat.

"Earthquake!" Jim's scream reached her as solid rock seemed to vibrate and hum.

Suddenly, Laura knew it wasn't thunder or earthquake, although thunder was closer to the cause. Laura had lived this horror before. So had Kurt. In the caves at Mesa Juanita. Trapped a mile below ground. Gallons of rain water from unseasonal squalls turned loose upon them.

"Kurt get out!" she screamed, already drenched in the first spray from the massive wall of water that had swept into the bend of the streambed behind her.

As the leading front of the water struck her and knocked the breath out of her, Laura was dismayed to see Kurt running not away from her but toward her in a futile, seemingly last-ditch effort to save her.

She reached for him, wanting his touch more than she'd ever pretended not to want it. But, as if a higher authority had heard her previous insistences that physical contact between Kurt and her was to be denied at all cost, they never touched, not even their fingertips. Her feet were knocked right out from under her, and the liquid enfolded her, smothered her, tried to drown her. She wanted air but breathed water instead, and the heavy fluid rushed into her protesting lungs. She choked, gagged, and gasped. Her sinuses burned, and her eyes stung.

She battled for her life against an inhuman assailant who had slipped up behind her and now held her in a suffocating embrace. She kicked and pummeled but couldn't connect. She grappled but couldn't take hold. It had form, it had mass: she felt them battering the life out of her. But it resisted her each and every attempt to fight back. It offered no eyes to gouge, no flesh to bite or scratch, no instep to stomp, no vital spots to knee or kick.

She ate more water and knew she was losing the battle.

Long-ago advice about drowning: relax and float. No relaxing or floating, though, in a maelstrom that waterlogged and held its victim under.

Her head hit something hard. Her leg scraped something hard. Her head hit again, and her ears rang as if cymbals had clanged inside them.

She held her breath, afraid her next hopeful gasp would force-feed more water. She had to have air, though, because her lungs demanded it, and her survival depended upon it.

"Aaaahhhhhh!" It was a scream of defiance, a refusal to surrender made on a long indraw of breath that gave her air as well as foam.

Her hip collided with something sharp, but the resulting pain seemed somehow inconsequential.

She wanted more air, but she was afraid to make another attempt, little encouraged by her last success.

She was submerged, in tepid, watery blackness. She felt for the hat on her head, but there was no longer a hat or miner's lamp. Knocked off?

She breathed—air. At the same time, she was swamped from behind.

Somewhere, she found a slippery handhold and pulled. Her face cleared its masking liquid. She tasted stale but delicious air even as the deluge swelled to reclaim her. Again, she defied it and fought her head free.

She swallowed some of the water and her stomach rebelled. She choked, coughed, and finally retched. All the while, she crawled on her bruised knees over submerged stone. She clawed and used tenuous handholds to keep her head above the rising flood.

"Kurt!" Where was he?

She looked up, but there was no dull light through vines and no crack seen from the bottom up. For the first time, she knew where she was. In the cave, and it was filling up. When it was topped with water, the stony grave would have her as its own, and there was nothing she could do about it.

She wasn't dead yet, though, because dead people didn't hurt: her body a massive aching, her head splitting, her lungs bursting.

Wasn't her life supposed to flash before her about now? She'd recalled more of it during her landing at the base camp. Now, she was too busy surviving to remember anything.

Her right boot found a shaky foothold on something that collapsed under her weight. She slid back beneath the waiting water, and her hair billowed, and her ears plugged.

She came up, her breathing reflexes completely out of sync. She had to concentrate to get them restarted: breathe in, out; inhale, exhale.

"Kurt!" She'd seen the concern and the fear in his eyes, his want and need to help her. In the end, not by her choice this time, she'd been forced to help herself.

She grasped the edge of a large stone and tugged herself

completely out of the water. Her soaked clothes were a ball and chain that she dragged along with her.

If she could get high enough, fast enough, and stay there long enough, she just might win. If only her eyes could adjust to the darkness so she could see — something, anything. As it was, she only heard the gallons of liquid in flux, water against stones, deadly fluid on the prowl.

"Ohhhhhh!" She'd hit the top of her head on a ceiling of solid rock. She could go no farther. She could only press her body lengthwise along the crease formed where the wall met ceiling and listen to the water as it searched for her.

She shouldn't be in this situation. Once burned should have meant forewarned. Past experiences were pointless if she didn't learn from them, and all of the warnings had been there: the thunder the night before, the slash marks of rain on the horizon, the fissure that stretched for miles in both directions, a puny stream hardly capable of having caused so much erosion on its own.

"Water is fluid," she reminded herself, the sound of her voice giving her comfort. "It can fall somewhere, pool behind an unstable dam of mud or logs or stones. The dam can break, and the water can barrel along impermeable rock for miles without stopping or diminishing. There doesn't even have to be a dam. A deluge of rain can convert to a veritable river in no time, commandeering some narrow gully or fissure in the ground." Laura remembered how surprised she'd been the first time someone told her how many people drowned each year in the deserts of the world.

The Amazon not being a desert had been what had fooled her. If the desert trained her to be on guard against many things, it never trained her for this. Nor was she consoled by how it had fooled Kurt, too.

She hated this place, knew its malicious intent, and should

have been on continual watch for whatever it threw her way.

"No!" she protested as water flowed around her feet.

Once gain, she tried to find a way around the rock above her. What irony if she survived this long only to perish beneath an overhang when the real ceiling was somewhere higher above.

Whether it was ceiling or overhang, it wasn't going to give her a way around it. She could only wedge herself more tightly against hard stone.

Water covered her feet, her hands, her arms, her legs, her torso.

She knew she had done everything she could on her own and so she prayed for help, for the strength to survive and for guidance to find a way. She ended with "Thy will be done."

When she opened her eyes, nothing seemed changed. The dials on her wristwatch were supposed to glow in the dark, but they didn't. The watch, supposedly waterproof, was battery-run, with no ticking parts, so she got no satisfaction from having rescued her-wrist-it-was-on from the water. She didn't know what time it was and could only count out the remaining seconds of her life: one-thousand-one, one-thousand-two, three hippopotamus, four hippopotamus . . .

Along with her one hand, her face was left free of the water, but the available air smelled dank.

She contemplated an underwater attempt to attain her freedom through the submerged cave entrance, but she didn't know where the entrance was or how far she'd been swept inside the possible tunnels and galleries. She might find her way out by swimming into the current, but the same current might prove too strong for her to force her way through.

Reminiscences intruded of the concern on Kurt's face as he tried to reach her, of his obvious horror when he'd spotted the glassy monster careening around the corner behind her.

Where had Kurt been taken on his steamroller ride? Common sense told Laura it hadn't been into the cave with her. He hadn't been positioned right. The water that had slapped her inside had probably been but an offshoot of the main flow which had swept Kurt along the major streambed. To his death? She refused to even think that!

A riptide effect pulled her and attempted to drag her back down the slanting rock and into deeper water. If the water was obviously in sudden retreat, it was still too much of a danger for Laura to thank her lucky stars. She was no safer than a bug floating in a washbasin from which the plug was suddenly pulled. The receding water was a death trap that could yet suck her down and under, and drown her.

The last of her immediate watery cocoon slid away with a clammy caress and an audible hiss. It left her drenched, completely spent, and cold. Her teeth chattered. There was an earthy, gritty taste on her tongue. Her heart beat wildly, accompanied by a drumbeat between her temples that was maddening in its intensity.

"Don't go into shock," she warned herself. "You're not home free by a long shot."

She struggled to get off her jacket and wring it of as much water as she could. She did the same with her blouse. She briskly rubbed her bare arms to increase deteriorating circulation. Her goose-bumped skin was like sandpaper, and her warming efforts irritated unseen bruises and cuts.

She struggled back on with her clothes, panicking when she thought she'd lost her jacket. Her mind flashed visions of water, like some inanimate monster in a Stephen King novel, come back to snatch it. She breathed relief when she found it, but she was disappointed when it, and her other wet clothes, offered nowhere near the warmth she wanted and required.

"What now?" she asked, and the sound of her voice obviously found more rocky surface off which to rebound than it had but minutes before.

Flushing sounds were louder.

For the moment, she pretended Kurt had been close enough, after all, to be swept into the cave with her. "Kurt?" she called. Only her echoes answered: "Kurt? Kurt? Kurt?"

She got colder and recognized the danger of hypothermia. She already had many of the symptoms: chills, disorientation, nausea, headache, lack of feeling in her limbs.

She slid slowly downward along the rock. Her feet tested the soundness of her route. She didn't want to slip off into oblivion at this stage of the game. "Game, more like war!" she said aloud.

She hoped to follow the withdrawing water through the most convenient and easily located exit.

There was an exceptionally loud gurgling, followed by a grumbling whoosh. Then, comparative silence.

"Hello!" she called, and her voice quivered. "Hello! Some-one! Anyone!"

Among the rebounding echoes was the familiar clicking of footsteps on stone.

"Laura!": a voice other than her own.

"Please, here!"

She wanted Kurt safe and sound. She wanted a miracle beyond the one that had saved her.

"Laura?"

A beam of light swept the damp surface of stone below her. A residue of mist danced in the reflecting light.

"Here," she said, and it was difficult to keep her voice calm. It was even more difficult for her to enunciate through chattering teeth.

She would have stood up and rushed to him, but her common sense prevailed. There were possibly unseen dangers still lurking in the dark: sharp stones, holes, deep pools. It wouldn't do to panic and carelessly break an arm or a leg.

"Are you all right, Laura?" It could be Kurt's voice, because the accoustics distorted. The trauma could have altered the timbre of his voice, as it made Laura's voice hardly seem her own.

"I think so," she put on a brave face. She was able to move, and her brain hadn't conked out altogether. On the other hand, she had once been seplunking with Tom Borocolis in Arkansas when he'd taken a nasty fall. He'd thought he was fine, too, and he had even walked all of the way out on his own, shock momentarily masking the pain of a pelvis stress-fractured in two places.

The light struck her full in the face. Her dilated and bloodshot eyes pained under the assault. Defensively, she threw up both of her hands. Blessedly, the light swerved elsewhere.

"Hold tight," the man behind the light said.

Loose rocks gave way somewhere, bounced, bounced again, rattled almost to a stop and plunked with audible splashes into an unseen puddle.

Laura drew up her legs, wrapped them with her arms, and hugged tightly.

"I thought you were a goner," he said and sat down beside her. He put her head on his shoulder, and said, "Thank God, you're safe."

"Kurt?" she asked.

"I was hoping he was safely in here with you," Jim said, giving her a consolatory squeeze.

Laura, who'd really known it was Jim all along, started to cry.

He sat holding her until she had control of herself. "Ready?"

She nodded in mute agreement.

He helped her to the harness and strapped her into it. He climbed the rope ahead of her and raised her into a night not nearly as dark as the darkness in the pit. He built a roaring fire, and she changed into dry clothes. She collapsed in the hammock nearest the fire.

How had she come to this, so battered and bruised, if not beaten, in the middle of a steaming wilderness, chilled to the bone in the bargain?

He made bouillon, a cup of which was hot in her hands. The soup was deliciously scalding all of the way down. She didn't miss the possible incongruity of pouring good liquid after bad.

"I should have anticipated," she said and didn't recognize her low, whispery voice. It contained a tremolo never there before. "Kurt and I, his father and mine, were once spelunking in some caves in New Mexico. I was very young at the time and foolishly tried to make it through an obviously too small crawlway. I got stuck. In the meantime, it started raining up top, a few miles away. Water could easily travel the distance and follow us into the hole, so we should have gotten out of there. Trouble was, everyone was busy trying to get poor Little Miss Stupid out of her predicament. During which time, water started rumbling like locomotives through the tunnels around us. It was like we had haphazardly staked ourselves out in a railroad yard, trains shooting by on equally random routes. Sooner or later, one of those trains was going to run us over. Except, they got me unstuck in time, and we took shelter on high ground in a large cavern. For twenty-four hours thereafter, these great surges of water periodically came flooding on through."

"Because of that, you think, all of these years later, you're supposed to know water dumped on rocky crags miles from here can locate an impermeable fissure in the ground and come barreling down on you? Come on, Laura, give yourself a break!" Jim argued.

"I should have known," she insisted.

"And Kurt should have known, too, by that same reasoning,

because he was in those same New Mexico caves with you, right? And I should have known because of what happened to me at Tenasco."

"What happened to you at Tenasco?" Laura asked over the rim of her cup. If he wanted her attention, he momentarily had it.

For the first time, she thought he looked haggard. His hair was mussed, he had a dirty streak across his left cheek, and he badly needed a shave.

"You think Kurt and you have the monopoly on being caught in the path of runaway water? Wrong! Two friends and I were hiking the old Spanish silver mines at Tenasco. The locale ring any bells?"

Laura shook her head. Nor was her ignorance anything unusual. The world was riddled with tunnels, caves, and caverns, every devotee having her or his favorites. She sipped more soup and wondered if she'd ever get warm again.

"Twenty-six-point-three miles south-southeast of Taxco. Extensive honeycombing of two whole mountains, the result of Aztec, Spanish, and finally Mexacali Minerali Company greed. Mined out by the time we got there: a playground for anyone with special permission and a penchant for hiking underground. No reported incidents or accidents to scare us off. Unfortunately for us, a weak ceiling of one shaft decided to collapse while we were in the neighborhood. What would normally have been no big deal suddenly became a very big deal with the reservoir some jerk bureaucrat had been bribed to authorize above ground on that very spot. Suddenly, a few hundred thousand gallons of water dropped through this hole, and we thought it was an earthquake, just like I thought this was an earthquake. So, don't tell me one time gives any carte blanche perspective needed to protect yourself from all repeats."

"I felt so helpless," Laura said weakly, unable to stifle a

shudder that accompanied the memory.

"You *were* helpless," Jim corrected and squatted so he was at eye level.

The firelight reflected off his tanned features and highlighted a handsomeness Laura hadn't really noticed in her preoccupation with Kurt. Although she knew how irrational it was, her sudden recognition of his good looks made her feel guilty and disloyal to Kurt. She shut her eyes in order to picture Kurt at his best. All she conjured for her efforts was his twisted expression of concern and horror when she'd last seen him. The memory was painful, and she needed the distraction Jim offered, so she quickly reopened her eyes.

"I know the helplessness of being at the mercy of a disembodied something that swallows you and refuses to cough you up," Jim assured. "The watery blackness. The horrendous roaring. The suffocating liquid. The bone-jarring collisions against hard, sharp stones."

"After awhile, I thought I was going to die," she confessed.

"Some do die," Jim said.

Laura's critical expression warned him away from saying anything whatsoever about the possibility of Kurt not coming through.

"My two friends died," Jim said, "and I don't know how I managed to survive. One second, I was gulping my last swallow of water, my lungs screaming out for air, and the next second, I was waking up, soaked and freezing cold, in a dark tunnel in the seeming middle of nowhere."

"I'm sorry about your friends," she consoled, but *Kurt couldn't be dead like they were.*

"I didn't think I'd get over the shock, and I didn't," he said and took her empty cup. "I did learn to live with it."

"Kurt isn't dead!" Laura insisted and, this time, said it aloud. It was very important to her that Kurt be alive, as if their separation, under such circumstances, had convinced her they had unfinished business between them.

Jim refused comment. "More soup?" he asked instead.

"Yes, please." She didn't press for his expanded opinion, because she didn't want to hear it.

He poured more bouillon into her cup from a pan whose bottom was black from hot coals. As he did so, it struck her how Kurt would be the one with her now if only it had been Jim with her in the trench. That, in turn, flooded her with guilt, because she didn't want Jim dead in Kurt's place. She just wanted Kurt alive, no strings attached. There *was* a difference.

She finished her second serving of soup in silence.

"A third cup of soup, or rest?"

"Rest," she decided.

"Things always look better after a night of sleep," he promised. "They, also, look better in the full light of a new day."

Laura suspected there were some things no amount of sleep, or no amount of sunny daylight, could make better. Nevertheless, she closed her eyes.

"Jim!" she exclaimed before he had time to move.

"I'm here, Laura."

She reached for his arm. "We are going to look for him?" she asked helplessly.

"Of course, we're going to look for him," he chided. His hand covered hers in a reassuring squeeze.

She didn't ask how many days they'd look, because she remembered the only one day they'd devoted to looking for Jean-Michael. Both Jim and Kurt had agreed that if one day didn't turn up anything, then, nothing would likely be turned up by any further efforts.

They traveled light, most of their gear stored at the campsite above the cave, and they searched a total of two-and-a-half days. It would have been three days, but Laura had needed time to adjust to the physical pain left by her harrowing experience, and Jim had used that first half a day to verify what Laura already knew: the cave was a dead-end, literally and figuratively. The speed with which it had filled with water, in accompaniment to Laura's struggles for survival, had hinted of only one entrance/exit and smallness: geological facts Jim soon verified. The absence of driftwood indicated just how powerful the riptides were that periodically cleaned the cavity. From all appearances, Laura might have been the first person ever in the place.

The uselessness of the cave as a means of pinpointing the last days of their fathers offered a doubly painful hurt for Laura, in that it meant Kurt, if dead, had died for nothing.

They followed the stream along its flow line, that being the route the deluge and Kurt had taken. They traveled inside the crack, because that was almost a roadway compared to the tangle of jungle above. It was like walking inside the barrel of a gun used by a madman for Russian Roulette, but they took the risk, because that's where they expected to find Kurt if he was capable of being found.

Once again, the fissure elicited comparisons to a gun barrel when it ended abruptly, its muzzle a small opening near the top of a high escarpment.

"I'm sorry, Laura," Jim said, a sympathetic arm around her shoulder. Then, he added, as if it might have escaped her, "There's no immediate access to down there from up here, except for the birds."

"And there's no way I can fool myself into believing Kurt survived getting shot out this end, is there?" she asked, and her voice caught in her throat. "It's a very long way down."

Standing on the lip of the abyss, field binoculars in hand, she surveyed the morass far below. The soupy combination of stagnant water, wiry bush, and snaggletooth trees had taken whatever had been fed it and had quickly made it its own.

Jim didn't say it was better this way, but Laura knew, as well as he did, that there was now no question that their search was over. Where Jean-Michael might have been left alive in the next gully, or behind the next tree, there were no such possibilities for Kurt. Had he survived drowning and the roller-coaster ride, he would have been killed by the fall. Had he survived the fall, he wouldn't have survived the swamp.

"Take a few minutes for yourself, Laura," Jim suggested and moved away into the jungle.

She would have preferred physical proof of Kurt's death, even if she could still shudder at the nightmare possibility of stumbling upon his corpse. A body would have left no loose ends, providing a finality that *might* allow a natural progression of mourning from beginning to middle to, most importantly, an end.

No *habeas corpus* meant a persistence of the question, "Yes, but what if . . . ?"

Laura knew from the painful experience of her father's disappearance, his body never found, that there was no final consolation or satisfaction for survivors in their holding onto such hope. She'd come here, all of these years after the fact, to put to rest just such what-ifs. All she'd done was saddle herself with more of the same.

All that was left was for her to get on with what brought her here to the Amazon in the first place. That was the least she could do for herself, because she needed something to keep her mind off Kurt and the better relationship they might have had if she'd not made such a concentrated effort to stifle it. It was the least she could do for Kurt, because he'd so desperately wanted his father proved innocent of crimes against humanity. It was the least she could do for Jim, because he'd stuck by her in the search for Kurt, even though he'd obviously expected the worst from the outset.

She turned and expected, from the sounds, to see Jim returning with more moral support. She was surprised to see he wasn't alone. As they walked toward her in shadow, their voices muted by low-key conversation, Laura's heart increased its rhythmic beat. Helplessly, she anticipated all of her fears proved wrong. By some miracle, this had to be Kurt returned, snatched from the brink of hell and given her by a Heavenly Father who knew how she now wished Kurt and she had another chance to explore the potential she'd been so afraid of. Such hope left her speechless and awash in emotions as drowning as any water had ever been.

She wanted to run to him, throw her arms around him, kiss him and know by the feel and taste of him that he was alive, but her legs wouldn't move.

5

Even when a stray shaft of sunlight illuminated, for just a fraction of a second, two heads of golden hair, Laura refused to surrender her need for Kurt's resurrection.

If Kurt weren't blond, trauma sometimes made hair change color overnight. If Kurt never had a disfiguring scar on his left cheek, why not one given him as proof of his ordeal? If Kurt was in his late thirties, and this man was obviously younger, then . . .

"Laura, this is Marc Klexter," Jim introduced as soon as the two stopped right in front of her.

Laura didn't want him to be Marc Klexter.

"Marc," she heard herself greet him, calmly. Obviously, some part of her operated independently of the chaos at loose inside her.

"He has word of Kurt, Laura," Jim said, and he must have known the effect that would have on her, because he took hold of her before adding, "he's alive."

She'd never doubted. "Alive?" she asked breathlessly, and her legs gave way. Yes, she *had* doubted!

Both men helped her to a natural bench formed by the rocky wall.

"Your hands are very cold, Marc Klexter," she told him and marveled at how dumb that sounded when she wanted to scream with joy, and most of all, thank God for the miracle. She'd said what she'd said only because she was so afraid she'd misheard. How many times, when she was younger, had she heard some strange man on the street, on a bus, in a park, and thought him her father come back to her?

If Marc's responding laughter sounded strained, Laura could chock it up to the mundaneness of her comment under the circumstances. "Cold hands, warm heart, Laura Lexly," he said but sounded less than convinced.

She shook her head to clear it. He was saying something—about Kurt?—and her mind was wandering.

". . . looked pretty bad, I'll have to admit. In fact, I figured he was breathing his last."

"You do mean Kurt?" Laura asked, because she had to be sure. "Kurt Reiger?" She wouldn't survive a malicious joke played by a sadistic man in a scar-face fright mask.

"That's what he says," Marc confirmed. "Dark hair. Violet eyes. Six-foot-one. Told me right where to find your camp above the cave. Although, he does remain a bit disoriented about some things. Can't seem to make up his mind whether or not Laura is dead."

"Where is he?" Laura asked, her heart pounding so loudly she could barely hear herself or anyone else. She was surprised they could hear her over the noise. She felt full and ready to burst, although it was more a filling of light helium than heavy water.

"He's at your camp above the cave. He insisted we head there as soon as he regained consciousness. Once there, we searched the cave. Swore he'd seen Laura swept inside it."

"He got that right," Jim confirmed. "It's a miracle she ever got out before she . . ."

"About Kurt," Laura interrupted. She didn't need or want to hear what she already knew about herself; it all paled before what Marc could tell her about Kurt.

"When we found nothing in the cave, he looked for a grave topside. Finding no grave, he cheered up. Said Laura must be alive, and the two of you, thinking him dead, had merely moved on. About then, I spotted your cache of food and equipment suspended by rope between two trees. Whether one or both of you had gone, you were obviously traveling light with plans of coming back. My guess was that you'd formed a search party. There'd been plenty of time between my hauling Kurt out of the trench, and his regaining consciousness, for you to have passed us by. So, here I am, having convinced him I could make better time in trying to find you if I did it alone."

"We've got to get to him," Laura insisted, standing. Unfortunately, she stood too fast, and it left her dizzy; it left Jim with the wrong impression — or, rather, the right one.

"We'll all be better rested in the morning," Jim insisted. As usual, Laura thought him gracious in the extreme to indicate they were all, not just she, suffering from exhaustion.

"I'm fine!" Laura argued.

"Maybe you're fine," he granted, "but I'm bushed, and Marc has come a good long way at a very fast clip. Besides, I think you should take the time to hear the rest of his good news."

"More?" Laura asked and disbelieved. Good news, she knew from bitter experience, was few and far between in this environment. If Kurt were alive, and she actually allowed herself to hope, that should have been all there was. Too much of a good thing made her suspicious.

She turned her full attention on Marc and told herself it wasn't his disfiguring scar that made her uncomfortable. If it were, she would feel guilty, embarrassed, and ashamed, because he couldn't help the way he looked. Laura had made it a point never to judge anyone before she delved beyond mere physical appearances, and she couldn't believe she was doing otherwise now. This young man had saved Kurt. He'd tramped alone, risking his life in the trench, to bring her the good news. It was thankless of her to see only his scar and to remember only how his cold touch gave her goose bumps.

"Marc's with the Universidad de Asuncion team at deNali," Jim said. "They found Jean-Michael."

"Jean-Michael?" Laura echoed. She sat down. Too much was coming at her all at once. A quesy feeling arose in the pit of her stomach, kept at bay only because she remembered how Jim had prefaced all of this with a promise of *good* news. "He's alive?"

"Yes, alive," Marc confirmed.

Tension drained out of Laura and left her as limp as a wet rag. She hadn't realized how much these last few days, since Jean-Michael's disappearance, had taken out of her. Hearing he and Kurt were safe did a lot to improve her well-being, but it didn't do nearly enough to replace the sheer mental and physical energy she'd expended on their behalf.

"Where's Jean-Michael been?" Laura asked. She still couldn't figure his disappearance.

She looked at Marc, determined to see the man behind the scar.

"I suspect he's been through hell," Marc said. "He was pretty well mauled when a couple of our group found him. He said he tangled with a jaguar, and I don't doubt it for a minute."

"He's going to be all right!" Laura said and made it a statement.

"That's our diagnosis," Marc agreed. "Of course, we radioed Captain Fortuna-Mata, with whom I believe you have a passing acquaintance. He's sending a doctor and a team to take Jean-Michael to the kind of facilities that can guarantee a complete recovery."

"Captain Fortuna-Mata asked Marc to check on us,' Jim said. "The captain tried to radio us as soon as the deNali team called him about Jean-Michael, but our radio was out."

"Jean-Michael insisted you were all okay when he left you," Marc explained. "However, the captain remained a little concerned, seeing as how you weren't receiving or broadcasting, so he asked one of us to check in with you to be sure. He gave me the coordinates for where your fathers supposedly dropped out of sight twenty-some years ago, or something like that?"

"Right!" Jim verified.

"Anyway, all's well that ends well. Yes?"

"Yes! Jim agreed.

"Amen," Laura intoned, and she figured she had a lot of prayerful thanks that needed saying. She started them off by giving a silent, quick one of thanksgiving. When she looked up, Marc was watching her.

Then and there, Laura realized it wasn't his scar that made her uneasy. In a strange way, that rugged remnant of some past violence actually bestowed him with a stark, masculine attractiveness.

It was his eyes she found so disquieting. If their jet-streaked emerald coloring was exquisite, they gave no suspicion of inner warmth nor any sense of readily definable emotion.

* * *

The next morning, on her way to meet Kurt, Laura was more nervous than when she'd walked the fissure in the other direction. It was as if the thought of Kurt waiting ahead made her more acutely aware of the odds for yet another flood to keep them apart — this time forever. It would have been just like this jungle to hold out hope and, then, perversely snatch it away. Therefore, with each hurried step Laura took, she listened for any sounds of approaching water, and she kept a constant vigilance for the fastest way up and out should a quick exit be necessary. She would have preferred traveling entirely above ground, but she knew most of the time expended in maneuvering the vegetation-clogged landscape would be time lost toward their reunion with Kurt — time lost toward Marc's reunion with his group at deNali. Besides, they did leave the natural sluiceway at night, none of them prepared to tempt fate by sleeping down there.

For the evening meal, Laura poured boiling water from one pot into a second pot that contained dehydrated lumps that would hopefully swell into a semblance of meat, potatoes, peas, corn, carrots and gravy; the label on the package had invitingly said "Beef Stew." She put the lid on the resulting brew, in accordance with instructions, and turned her attention to Jim who took a seat on a log across from Marc who sat with his back against a tree.

"Dueling?" Jim asked, his question obviously directed at Marc, and Laura thought she'd misheard. Considering where they were, and what they were about, Laura didn't understand the question.

Marc, though, was faster on the uptake. The young man — Laura estimated he was somewhere in his twenties — raised his right hand to his face and gently ran fingertips along the length of his scar. "You mean sabers, swords, rapiers, and foils?" he asked and flashed a smile that had all the right ingredients but somehow fell flat; Laura decided it was his eyes that were to blame: they had no inner sparkle.

In fact, his eyes were the exact color of a large chunk of beryl Laura once saw displayed at the Bogota Gold Museum. "Largest uncut emerald in the world!" her guide had proclaimed, and Laura had seen cold green stone, massively flawed by inclusions, that only reflected light; it had none of its own.

"Do people still duel?" Laura asked, still not sure Jim's query had been serious. Frankly, she was surprised he'd so blatantly catered to his curiosity. Bringing up Marc's disfigurement for discussion hardly seemed the gentlemanly thing to do.

"Dueling is illegal everywhere, isn't it?" Marc asked and seemed far less concerned by the subject than Laura suspected she would be in his shoes. "Then again, I do believe there are still hold-over secret dueling societies, usually military-connected, usually in Germany. Yes? However, I also believe even dueling in those is nowadays more a stereotypical ritual, padding provided to prevent serious injury."

"Padding provided, except for certain areas of the face," Jim said, and he sounded as if he knew what he was talking about.

"The face?" Laura queried with a shiver. Her face was one of the first places she'd want covered. Didn't fencers wear masks?

"The theory, held by die-hards, being, I suppose, that one spot has to be vulnerable, or the whole purpose of the duel becomes moot?" Marc ventured and didn't sound all that sure. "Besides which, I suspect, it's a general misconception, held by participants, that a facial scar becomes a decided badge of 'macho.' "

"You don't hold with that theory?" Jim asked, and Laura, who suspected the stew was done, left cooking long enough to continue following the conversation.

"Can a scar like mine ever make one more attractive?" Marc evaded. "Maybe Laura would be so kind as to make that judgment. Laura?" He turned the scarred side of his face toward her.

Laura felt awkward and looked away. She took hold of the lid on the stew pot and burned her hand in the process. It took all of her self-control not to cry out from the pain.

"There you have the answer," Marc assumed. "Few beautiful women are really turned on by men's scars. Why, then, willingly burden oneself with such an obstacle when courting?"

Actually, Laura had been so ill at ease because she'd not known how to tell him that she thought he might have been too beautiful — for a man — without the distraction the scar offered. His features were too perfect, otherwise. His skin was too blemish-free, his tan too golden. His physique was too much the embodiment of some usually unattainable goal, like the Greek sculptures of Polycleitus which represented not real men but mathematical ideals. Unlike the copy of Polycleitus' "Athlete" in the National Museum at Athens, Marc was saved from sterile otherworldliness by his one glaring imperfection.

"In truth, this —" And his fingertips once again outlined the scar in its right-to-left diagonal across his left cheek. "— Is the result of my quite unintentional run-in with *Crataegus callipruellis,* more commonly known hereabouts as 'Crown of Jesus.' The story goes that when local Indians were first introduced by early Catholic missionaries to the Passion of Christ, the new converts believed His crown of thorns had to be Brazilian-grown."

"A thorn did that?" Laura asked and tried not to make "that" sound as horrendous as he obviously mistook her notion of it.

"In nineteen-eighty-four," Marc said. "October. I was being

lowered over the side of a cliff not too far from here for samples of *Perludium sud-Americanus,* a moss, a liverwort really; quite rare and quite beautiful, myriad asterisk-like yellow and white flowers. The rope broke: an inherent factory flaw. A cliff-grown thorn bush cushioned my fall, saved me, and extracted this as its price for its good deed. However, rest assured that plastic surgery will solve the problem. I'd be under the skillful scalpel of Dr. Joseph Faxner, at this very moment, if science hadn't called me back to the Amazon Basin."

Laura tried to imagine the scar surgically removed, and she was tempted to tell him not to bother. Most of what she found attractive in any man had a lot to do with individual imperfections. Take Kurt, for instance. He was ever-so-slightly bowlegged. He had a small mole that she only now remembered on the underside of his chin. He had an S-shaped scar in the crook of his arm, opposite his left elbow.

"You were here in October of nineteen-eighty-four?" Jim asked.

"It's not likely I'd forget," Marc said and nodded thanks to Laura who'd filled a cup with stew and handed it to him. "Under the circumstances—" he added and touched his scar again.

"I was here in October of eighty-four," Jim said and made it sound like an accusation.

"Oh?" Marc asked and sounded surprised. "But, then, the world is full of such coincidences, no?"

"As now, I was looking for some trace of my father," Jim said and took the cup of stew Laura offered without looking at it or at her. "Have you heard of my father: Daniel Kenner?"

"Daniel Kenner," Marc echoed. He took a bite of stew, chewed reflectively and said, "No, I don't believe I have. Should I?"

Laura eyed Jim curiously. If she didn't know better, she'd

think Jim was giving Marc the third degree.

"Then again," Marc reconsidered, "Captain Fortuna-Mata might have mentioned him when he gave me coordinates to find you. But, no—" He took another healthy bite of stew. "—I don't believe he did."

"What brings you back?" Jim asked, and Laura watched him over the rim of her cup which billowed steam.

"Same as before," Marc said and seemed content to leave it at that.

"Mosses and liverworts?" Jim pressed.

"One particular moss," Marc obliged and punctuated with another hearty spoonful of the same stew Laura found almost unpalatable. His spoon scraped empty parts of the metal container, and Laura anticipated his asking for seconds; she signaled he was more than welcome to them. His response was to lean toward her and hand over his nearly empty cup. Laura touched his fingers during the exchange and found them, especially compared to the warmth of the aluminum, as cold as ever.

"What moss?" Jim asked, and, once again, Laura heard it as something more than small talk; she wished she knew what was coming off—if anything.

"*Gurillinicum perlkikus* to be scientific-specific," Marc said and stretched for the refill Laura had ladled for him. He took a spoonful, chewed the results with an expression that insinuated savory meat, not cardboard-equivalent, and said, "Haven't seen any of it around here, have you? Gray-blue color, whispy strands like a very old man's beard, and parasitically attached to low-growing limbs and branches."

He paused, as if he expected them to surprise him with a "Yes!" So expectant did he seem that Laura felt obliged to say, "No, I don't believe I've seen any of it."

"Pity," Marc concluded. "We could really use a helping hand about now, and a bit of luck is always appreciated. Poor

Professor Denlick has possibly found his one real chance for renown, and it's slipping through his fingers."

"Professor Denlick?" Laura echoed, took another spoonful of stew and decided she might finally be ready to attempt eating monkey if anyone would offer; the captain had once mentioned Professor Denlick, in passing.

"I was here with him in eighty-four," Marc said. "We gathered plant samples in anticipation of the day these rain forests are no more. You know how many acres of this gets wiped out a year?" He shook his head to emphasize: "It's unbelievable! The equivalent to one of your fifty states: Connecticut, I think; maybe California.

"Progress it's called, but it wipes out whole species of plants that might provide the world with the next miracle cure. Quinine came out of tree bark. Chaulmoogra oil from the kalawa tree treats leprosy. It's hard for the professor to accept the reality of some peasant farmer, clearing off a plot of land that won't ever produce a life-subsistence level, slashing and burning the last plant on earth that might cure a modern disease."

Laura was fascinated. Jim, on the other hand, appeared to lose interest. He finally attacked his cooling stew with a vengeance that made him resemble someone out to win a who-can-eat-stew-the-fastest contest.

"There's a graduate student at the University of Maryland who pulled this moss, long-dead and dried, out of a storage drawer last year, quite by accident, and did some experimenting with it. Seems a chemical concoction he distilled from it can do unusual things to the human immune system. Nothing conclusive, though, because we hadn't brought back enough. So, here we are, in greater force, looking for more — without much success."

"Fascinating," Laura admitted.

"Oh, it certainly is that!" Marc agreed but lacked the enthusiasm Laura expected.

There remained something about this scarred student, on his mission of mercy in the Amazonian wild, that should have elicited a far greater emotional response than he was getting from Laura—or, at least, Laura thought so. Then again, there were some people, and she had run across a few in her time, who just didn't have the magic to push any of the right buttons.

"Hold the dirty dishes, and I'll wash them when I return," Marc said, laid his cup aside and stood. He chose the most direct route into the privacy afforded by the bordering jungle and took it.

"What was that all about?" Laura asked after he'd disappeared.

"Oh," Jim answered. "I was merely curious about his scar. I took fencing in college under a German master who had one almost exactly like it. Very proud of it, too, was Herr Klaus. He thought it made him irresistible to women; and, you know, from what we envious students saw, he was apparently right; which makes you somewhat of an exception to his rule. At the time he had us all wishing for scars just like his."

"That's it?" Laura asked when he was obviously prepared to leave it at that.

"That's it!" he confirmed. "Sorry to disappoint you."

The only thing that disappointed and disturbed her was her intuitive feeling that his that's-it concession wasn't all of it at all.

"Here!" Marc said that next afternoon, succinctly paraphrasing Brigham Young when the Prophet indicated the Salt Lake valley as Zion for the saints in his charge.

Jim and Laura stopped, as if on command, both curious by Marc's pronouncement. By their estimation, they had a good ways yet to go.

"It's where I found Kurt," Marc elucidated; Laura noted he didn't boast it as a "rescue."

Laura surveyed her immediate surroundings and recognized the decidedly tight S-curve of the fissure from her first time through in the opposite direction.

"I was topside," Marc continued, "without the faintest notion any of this was here." Laura recalled how easily Kurt and she had been fooled into thinking the covering vines were solid ground. "All of a sudden," Marc said, "it's like an earthquake. Water geysers out of the ground, apparently having had trouble getting around these bends as easily as it rushed down the straightaway into them. The result was spray every which way; and, suddenly, someone washed out of the hole like a ship-wrecked sailor."

"Kurt," Laura identified to herself and gave thanks again that he'd been spit up here, rather than spit over the drop-off at the trench's far end. She shuddered at how one S-curve made the difference between a joyous and a tragic end. The luck of the draw gave her a queasy feeling.

"Hard to believe there was enough water in here to overflow," Marc said, his head thrown back to survey the top a good ways up.

"Oh, not all that hard, believe me!" Laura contradicted.

"Amen to that," Jim confirmed.

Later on, confronted by yet another bend in the streambed, they were once again brought up short, but this time not by Marc.

"Hear that?" Laura asked, unsure if Jim and Marc had heard, too, or had stopped because she did.

"I do indeed," Marc informed. "It's known as dinner."

"Dinner?" Laura asked over her loud-pounding heart.

"A peccary, by the sounds," Marc identified. "One evidently

in distress. Frankly, I'm surprised we haven't found more dead and injured animals, this pit is a natural catch-all. No doubt, it'll become more cluttered between now and the next big flush."

"Think one of us should check it out?" Jim asked, and Laura didn't want to be the first around the corner.

"I'll go," Marc volunteered, as if it were already a foregone conclusion.

Did scarred men find it necessary to compensate for their disfigured good looks the way some short men seemed compelled to perform he-men excesses?

"They can be quite irritable," he said and sounded like an authority.

"Please do be careful!" Laura begged and was rewarded with an expression that said, "Lady, someone who has the wherewithal to volunter for this kind of duty is certainly competent enough to carry it off safely." Without a word, he'd made Laura, who only wished him well, feel put-down and embarrassed. That knack was one more thing about him that she found less than endearing.

If she wished, only in passing, that the peccary could get in one glancing blow — only enough to draw the tiniest amount of first blood to prove Marc less than invincible — her ungracious flight of fantasy was short-lived. The last thing anyone needed in this environment was a wound that could go septic. The perpetual heat and humidity could make even the most insignificant of scratches explode into long-lasting, ugly, festering lacerations. So what that Marc had so little evident charisma? He'd originally had so much in the looks department, it was only fair he came short-changed in something.

Weapon drawn, Marc began a slow stalk around the bend. Jim and Laura drew their revolvers in backup; Laura only knew hers worked, after its dunking with her in the fissure and cave, because she'd made it a point to clean and test-fire it since the incident. Marc moved with the cool confidence of someone who knew what he was about. Laura thought he'd just as readily know what steps to take on an overcrowded life raft: chuck some people overboard. Then, she caught her derogatory thoughts in time. After all, Marc had already proved his compassion by rescuing Kurt. If the water had done its part and up-chucked Kurt — the whale hadn't done better with Jonah — Marc had been there with artificial respiration and CPR. In addition, he'd made the extra effort to track down Jim and Laura.

The interrupting gunshot was loud: bounced off narrow perimeters. A reflexive jerk of Laura's index finger almost pulled the trigger of her revolver, and she thanked whatever lucky stars saved her from that embarrassment.

"All clear!" Marc called confidently.

"Maybe we should ask him to join us permanently and handle all such little chores?" Jim suggested.

Laura couldn't tell if he were serious, but she hoped not. Too much of Marc, she was sure, would wear mighty thin. "I'm sure he's as anxious to get on with his business as we are to get on with ours."

Marc's gun was holstered, his knife drawn, when they joined him. "His taste won't hold a candle to a domestic pig. However, he will offer an attractive alternative to beef stew."

"Tell me about it!" Jim confirmed.

Laura, in the meantime, thought there was something to be said, from her city-born-and-bred standpoint, for ignorance being bliss. She preferred cellophane-wrapped chops, cutlets, and pork loin. Besides, there was something about the way Marc obviously relished his task that Laura found unhealthy, although she was sure there were legions of macho hunters who'd vehemently argue the point.

She moved further upstream and pretended interest in geological striations along one rock face.

When the meat was displayed on a spit over their evening fire, the resulting smell, savory in the extreme, did whatever additional brainwashing was necessary to have Laura made ready and eager for her first crackling piece of the meat, skillfully sliced off by Marc and, fire-roasted, laid on her plate. Her first bite was pure heaven. Her second bite was almost as good. Even the unladylike lickings of her fingers in finale were a pleasure enjoyed.

Obviously as satiated as Laura, Marc stretched out by the edge of the fire. Jim disappeared into the privacy of the nearby woods. Marc's hands were locked to pillow his head, his glass-like green eyes focused on the weave of leaves and vines overhead.

Laura conjectured how Jim and Marc, two blond-haired, green-eyed men, each with a nose, a mouth, ears, a chin, a neck, a trunk, arms, and legs could turn out so different in end result—inside and out; not that either was unattractive in his own right.

When the gaze of Marc's cold, green eyes shifted to surprise and locked with Laura's, she shivered at a sensation clearly reminiscent of when she'd stared down the drooling jungle cat.

"You actually like this jungle," she said, because the discomforting moment demanded small talk to make it seem bearably mundane.

"Like it?" he replied as if her accusation genuinely perplexed him. "No," he paused. "I don't exactly like it. No more than I'd necessarily like any other place to which I was assigned for a job. One merely makes the best with what one is given, doesn't one? Like you do. Like Jim does. Like Kurt does."

"Did I hear my name?" Jim asked and stepped from the shadows to reclaim his vacated spot by the fire.

"Actually, Laura was telling me how anxious she is to see Kurt again," Marc said: and, if it wasn't a lie that she was anxious to see Kurt, it *was* a lie that she'd just confided any such thing to Marc.

"Did she tell you how inordinately fond she's become of him?" Jim asked with a mischievous smile. "I think it has all indications of blossoming into something serious before this is all over."

"Oh?" Marc responded, his eyes back on Laura, his lips smiling a smile that portrayed something other than humor.

"Nonsense!" Laura insisted. Where she might have privately admitted to Jim that, despite all of her efforts to make it otherwise, he was possibly right in his assessment, she was loathe to so expose her inner feelings to Marc. No matter what Marc had done for them, and he'd admittedly done a lot— No matter what he might yet do for them—Laura simply didn't like him, and there it was: all spelled out! Not knowing how, she'd come to see him as she saw the jungle: something with a seductively beautiful but distorted facade that concealed just beneath its surface an unpleasantness not altogether easily identifiable.

Another bend: the next-to-the-last, as far as Marc, Jim, and Laura were concerned. Beyond it, a long straightway to the cave. Thoughts of the cave still gave Laura goose bumps.

"Won't be long!" Jim congratulated. "Nor will I be sad to say final good-byes to this hole in the ground."

Laura's agreement went without saying. However, her present frame of mind revolved more around Kurt. What they'd shared certainly put them beyond a mere good-to-see-you-again handshake. On the other hand, could she trust herself, even now, to risk the more appropriate thank-God-you're-alive hug?

In the end, it was Kurt's impatience to see Laura, not vice versa, that took the decision out of her hands. Having started out to meet her, he was just around that next-to-the-last bend when she got there.

"Kurt!" Laura exclaimed and succumbed to impulse: took the steps that separated them, slid her arms around his waist, laid her head against his chest, heard the speedy beat of his heart, and said: "Do you know how very very glad I am to see you?"

All Kurt knew was that he was so glad to see Laura — he had no qualms whatever about enjoying the sudden slippage in her defenses. When he'd seen that massive wall of water snatch her from him, all he could think was how unfair life was. His thoughts of death, and many accompanied his life-threatening ride, always included Laura. Whenever he'd grown tired of struggling, he'd rallied with thoughts that Laura just might survive.

It had something to do with the way she looked, the way she smelled, the way her skin felt against his fingertips. If he was sympathetic to the complications her mother offered, and if he'd been won over by Laura's frankness in spelling out her fears, not to mention his wanting to make everything easy for her, he simply didn't have the willpower *not* to want: to hold her hand, to touch her face, to run his hand along the exquisite line of her neck.

"Laura," he spoke her name: ambrosia on his tongue. "Laura, Laura, Laura."

For the moment, it didn't matter that what was happening wouldn't necessarily do either of them any good. It didn't matter that his father alive in Argentina would make June Lexly's hate-besotted suspicions detrimentally valid. It didn't matter that what he had to offer might never compensate Laura for her father murdered and her mother estranged.

Or, did it matter?

He tightened his arms around her, and Laura wondered what he was thinking. Did he know what barriers had cracked inside her when she'd thought him lost forever? Not even she, until now, had known how complete the breach. Did he know she'd mourned not only him but the passing of any chance to explore the potential feelings she'd denied? Did he know how afraid she was to let her now-released emotions run rampant when they didn't necessarily have her best interests at heart?

There was no denying his body felt good pressed tightly against her. There was inexplicable joy in the hardness of his back against her palms, in the way he trembled when her fingers slid up the back of his neck and buried in the curly dampness of his hair. *She* trembled in that joy!

"A handshake will do just fine for me," Jim said and reminded Laura that Kurt and she weren't alone.

Reluctantly, she pulled back. This time, though, it was different from all the other times. This time her hands refused to come free; they lingered on his arms as if glued there. What's more, she didn't want them free. She luxuriated in whatever it was that pulsed, unseen, from Kurt's body to her own, from his arms to her hands.

She started to cry. Whether from sadness or in joy, she couldn't be sure. She wanted it to be for joy, but . . .

"Laura, Laura," Kurt consoled and renewed their embrace. He didn't want her hurt by whatever these emotions were flailing between them. He just couldn't help the way he felt. Didn't she know how hard he'd fought against this happening? Guiltily, he suspected he hadn't fought nearly hard enough.

"I don't know about the rest of you, but I'd like to shed this hole as quickly as possible," Marc impatiently said, and Laura heard no sympathy there: no appreciating her tears as a catharsis to make her feel better.

"I think we can spare them a minute or two more," Jim argued, and there, thought Laura, was the difference between one blond, green-eyed man and the other: understanding compassion.

If Laura let Kurt dry her eyes, it wasn't to oblige Marc's anxiousness to get a move on. It was because her tears had run their course, served their purpose. She now felt better able to cope.

Kurt's hands parenthesized her face. His thumbs caressed her still-damp cheeks. At the same time, he sensed Marc's unease but couldn't understand it. There was a lot about the young man he couldn't fathom. Having been saved by Marc didn't make Kurt know him.

His patience apparently stretched beyond its limits, Marc headed off alone to find the rope Kurt had left for them to climb free.

"I know the kid saved your life, Kurt," Jim said under his breath, "but is he, *or is he,* somewhat of a cold fish?"

"He is that," Kurt diagnosed, his head bowed, his words converted to a light breeze in Laura's hair.

Once sure Marc wasn't looking back—as if his doing so would taint what she was about to do, Laura put a hand to each side of Kurt's face, lifted her weight on her toes and kissed him. Her mouth didn't linger against his, though, because the resulting heart-stopping shock that punched her emphasized her audacity and the inherent implications of what she'd done.

"Maybe you'd prefer I join Mr. Cold Fish?" Jim ventured with a well-didn't-I-predict-this? tone of voice.

"Don't you dare!" Laura protested and extended an arm to include him in a three-way hug. She wondered what Kurt thought, after all her fine talk about keeping their relationship safely neutral?

"Maybe we *should* get out of here," Kurt suggested. Laura's closeness and her kiss had had their effects, and he wanted time to analyze this latest development. He hoped it was a permanent loosening of her defenses; however, if it were, that gave him pause: a sudden sense of personal responsibility to make sure he'd not persuaded her into something they'd both live to regret. He'd felt safer when she was in opposition, two heads to consider the consequences. Now, she seemed more vulnerable and in need of his protection — against him and his runaway desires.

"It would be just like this jungle to send another flash flood to wash us all away," Laura observed pessimistically. Yes, she wanted out of this hole in the ground and finally understood Marc's chagrin at the delay.

Jim, though, was inclined toward optimism. "The jungle owes us," he said. "It's about time it paid off."

"Agreed," Kurt said, "but life is seldom fair." If it gave something to him, even this temporary happiness with Laura, he had to watch for a sneak attack from his rear.

They joined Marc in the campsite above the cave. He'd made cocoa while he waited. "I've made plenty," he assured and finished off his. He leaned for his backpack which he'd discarded. "Now, happy reunions made —" Laura thought she heard sarcasm. "— I must get back to my own."

"Surely, you'll stay for something to eat besides cocoa!" Jim protested.

Even Laura, who was probably the least disappointed to see Marc go, had to agree with Jim: "A good meal, a good sleep, a fresh start in the morning?"

"I think not," Marc resisted. "There's still a lot of daylight left, and I can make good time. My companions, if they've had as lousy luck since I left as they did when I was there, will welcome another set of eyes."

"I think you should reconsider," Kurt said, obliged to give his two-cents' worth. He had the uncanny feeling Marc disapproved of Laura's show of emotion in the fissure and was fleeing in the face of it. If that were the case, Kurt felt sorry for him.

"I shall radio Captain Fortuna-Mata that you are happy and well," Marc said, apparently no more prepared to accept Kurt's invitation than the others.

He shook hands, his hand icy cold when it briefly took hold of Laura's fingers and released them. Somehow, without saying, he gave the distinct impression that he'd have preferred dispensing with even that minor formality.

After the time Marc and she had spent together, Laura still couldn't bring herself to offer a farewell hug, if just because she sensed he wouldn't welcome it.

Did he dislike her because he sensed her dislike of him?

"Once again, thanks for pulling me out of the drink," Kurt appreciated, not for the first time.

"Anything to help the cause," Marc dismissed. "Good luck, by the way."

"And if you're ever in Portland, you'd better not pass through without looking me up," Kurt warned.

"Done!" Marc assured and left without further delay.

There was no doubt about the palpable relief Laura felt when he was gone, even if she couldn't put a definition to it. "Dinner is on me!" she announced to Jim and Kurt who still looked perplexed by Marc's hasty departure. "What'll it be?"

"I had 'Beef Stroganoff' last night," Kurt commented. Something about Marc bothered him, and he wondered why. Beyond his striking, scarred good looks and his apparent disapproval of Laura's outward expressions of emotion, there was something disturbing.

"Chicken Rice Pilaf?" Laura suggested, determined to remove the chill left by Marc's departure.

"I hoped to have fresh capybara for your arrival," Kurt said and turned his attention back to Laura who, more than Marc, deserved it. "Unfortunately, the only game in town seems to be monkey."

"Before last night, I might have succumbed even to monkey," Laura confessed. "However, last night, we had peccary."

"Lucky you!" Kurt complimented, then jokingly added: "I suppose you never thought to bring me a slab of bacon?"

"Small peccary," Laura alibied. "With hardly a morsel left for the raiding party of greedy ants that quickly took up where we left off."

Obviously not as easily distracted by Laura or the prospect of food, Jim asked: "Do you think Marc is all there? Up here, I mean?" he added with a tap of his right temple. "I know he seems in his element when he's lobbing all that botanical double-talk, but . . ." He shrugged and changed the subject: "Did someone say we're having monkey for dinner?"

"Not unless they've changed the ingredients of 'Chicken Rice Pilaf,' " Laura corrected. Only because she'd banqueted on peccary the night before did she find her culinary efforts of that afternoon edible.

After which, a group effort cleaned up the dishes.

Jim retired to a nearby spot to sharpen his knife.

Kurt joined Laura against a tree and helped her unfold her map of the area. The map, despite their combined attention, ended upside down. "We do make a well-coordinated pair, don't we?" Laura observed light-heartedly and gave the half turn necessary to put it right. She took out her Eversharp; Jim had written warning of how ink in pens expanded in the heat and invariably exploded on unsuspecting clothing. She began to trace her estimation of the fissure on the printed landscape. "In case I'm ever back in this neighborhood," she joked.

Laura's penciling stopped well short of completion.

"I thought it would be longer," Kurt observed astutely and moved closer.

"Here's where Marc said he pulled you to safety," Laura

said, and her pencil tapped the spot where she'd interrupted her drawing.

"I'd say he got it about right," Kurt agreed. "Of course, it's hard to tell when dealing with the artwork of an amateur topographer."

Laura appreciated his wit even though she had something on her mind that kept her from responding in kind. "And, here's where we're headed," she said, and her pencil slid to another spot on the map. "While over here—" And away went the pencil. "—are the caves at deNali."

"Whoever said you couldn't read a map?" Kurt asked. "Jim, did you say Laura couldn't read a map?"

"Not I!" Jim denied but didn't look up. He breathed on the surface of his knife blade and watched the accumulation of moisture dissolve into the distorted reflection of his face on the steel.

"So, if Marc was at deNali—" Laura wouldn't join in the fun as long as she had something so serious to say. "—when Captain Fortuna-Mata radioed him the coordinates to take him here—" She drew the most direct line to their fathers' last campsite. "—how did he end up way over here—" Her pencil detoured to the far end of the partially drawn fissure line. "—to fish you out of the drink?"

6

Brought in for consultation, Jim frowned, shrugged, and arbitrated: "We all know, from personal experience, that the shortest distance between two points in this terrain is not necessarily a straight line."

"What kind of a feasible line, crooked or straight, puts Marc all of the way over here when the flash flood struck?" Laura punctuated with a pencil-jab to the map that put a hole in the waterproof paper.

"Maybe he got lost?" Jim suggested.

"Did Marc remind you of someone apt to get lost?" Laura asked, frustrated by Jim's unlikely but logical solutions.

"Where Marc picked me up was a bit off the beaten path, Jim, if he were headed for our fathers' last campsite," Kurt came to Laura's defense. "Even if he were lost, would he have wandered quite so far off the most direct route from deNali?"

"So, just what is it you two would like me to say?" Jim asked with a raised eyebrow. "More than: 'It would probably be easy for Marc to explain if he were here'?"

Laura wasn't sure what she wanted Jim to say. She just didn't like the apparent anomaly. She tried for another: "The botanists are at deNali. Somehow, a badly wounded Jean-Michael makes it to deNali. The botanists find him and radio Captain Fortuna-Mata. The captain asks one of them to contact us. Marc agrees. He sets out and gets lost. He fishes Kurt out of the drink. He comes after us. Two-plus days later, he finds us. So, how does all of that happen within the course of a mere five days of Jean-Michael disappearing from our monkey-bake? Just to cover the distance between here and deNali, one-way, takes four days. Joe went back to the runway because it was as close as the caves. Right?"

"Who says the botany team was at deNali when they found Jean-Michael?" Jim asked with more maddening logic. "DeNali is just their base camp, like the runway is ours, right? Maybe they were out reconnoitering, farther afield, closer to here when they stumbled on Jean-Michael. They had a radio with them. They called Captain Fortuna-Mata. He gave Marc the coordinates. Marc headed this way, got sidetracked, for whatever the reason, and ended up at the right place, at the right time. Should we look a gift-horse in the mouth?"

Jim's explanation worked, but Laura wondered if it worked nearly enough.

"Look, Laura," Jim reasoned. "So, you don't like Marc . . ."

"Who said I don't like him?" she interrupted, then remembered this was the man who'd foreseen Kurt and her as interested before she'd ever accepted that possibility herself.

"I'm not all that fond of him, myself, if the truth were known," Jim said and didn't bother to debate her likes or dislikes. "I do think it's only fair, however, that we keep all of this in perspective, remembering that if Marc were indeed this ill-intentioned mystery man of ours who — by the way — we now know wasn't responsible for Jean-Michael's disappearance, why didn't he just give Kurt a little push and let him wash away?"

"I'm not accusing Marc of anything!" Laura defended, although that wasn't altogether true. Once he was out of sight, she was back to imagining eyes in every shadow. Had her paranoia diminished when Marc was near, or had the watching only seemed that much closer? She'd been so concerned about Kurt's welfare, at the time, she'd shoved everything else, voyeur included, into the back of her mind — until now. "I only thought one of you might enlighten me on points I find odd."

"And, I only wish you'd thought of these oddities while the only person likely to answer them to everyone's satisfaction was around to do so," Jim dismissed and went back to the spot he'd occupied prior to his summons.

Laura bit her lip and accepted the hug Kurt gave her in consolation. She laid her head on his shoulder and admitted: "Jim is right about one thing: I don't much care for Marc Klexter."

'Oh?" Kurt asked, and he sounded surprised; Laura suspected he was really as aware of her dislike as Jim was.

She waited for him to say something more. When he didn't, she rationalized for him: "It's unsporting to expect the rescued man to venture anything derogative beyond, 'Marc's an admitted cold fish!'?"

"I think that's a fair assumption," Kurt confirmed. In truth, as ungrateful as it might be, he didn't care for Marc, either, possibly because he was such a cool customer. Kurt didn't require any man to wear his emotions on his sleeve, but he liked some indication of something beneath the surface. The only emotion he'd suspected of Marc, and that negative, was his apparent impatience with Laura's tears.

"I am glad he saved you, though," Laura admitted and put her hands over Kurt's large fingers that curved one side of her waist. "Although, now that he has, we have to have another long talk, like the one we had above the treetops."

"Right now?" he asked and knew he needed more time to prepare, more time to get his thoughts in order. Up to now, he'd been spending too much time enjoying to ruin it with any more in-depth analysis of what it all could mean.

He needn't have worried, though, about any rushed timetable. If anyone needed more time to analyze what was happening and what might happen, it was Laura. "No, not right now," she assured. "Somewhere up the line, though. For now I'll risk riding the flow, even if it is carrying me along at just about the same breakneck speed of the wave that socked me into that cave."

"Welcome to the roller-coaster ride, lady!" he said and, knowing just how she felt, placed a tender kiss among her golden hair.

Kurt had used his time, while waiting for the return of Marc with Jim and Laura, to check out the area for the sedimentary limestone which had brought them looking in the first place. He had no good news to report for his efforts, and no one felt it necessary to waste more time at the detour site.

The morning after Marc's departure, the remaining three set off on the quickest route to their fathers' last campsite. Their route, as Jim could have pointed out, had he been so inclined, was hardly a straight line. Their constant weave around this obstacle or another, through this vegetation-rioting stretch of underbrush or another, up this hill and around this gully, had Laura daydreaming of the comparative freeway comfort of the fissure. Of course, there was little danger of being washed away by rampaging floods, but it rained twice in a four-hour period, then rained again at lunch. They opted to eat trail bars rather than cook in the downpour, another bland concoction rescued from yet another vacuum-sealed packet.

That afternoon, when Jim called a halt, Laura was ready for the rest. She plopped on a rock suspiciously convenient, wiped perspiration from her weary brow, eyed a nearby pond and entertained fantasies of plunging on in, then asked: "Anyone want to venture how much farther?"

"Sure," Jim volunteered; Laura waited expectantly. "We're here!"

"You're kidding!" Laura responded automatically and refused to believe him. Not because she didn't trust they'd covered enough mileage—she felt as if she'd just walked nonstop, New York to San Francisco; but, the place didn't have the "feel" she expected. There was no "sense" of her father having ever been here. There was no "sign" that this was *the* place. Where was the psychic-something Jim had led her to believe would accompany the three of them being here? This place could have been any of a thousand such places passed during their trek to get here.

"Never know, would you?" Jim observed, and Laura thought that a gross understatement. "On the other hand, it has been twenty-four years."

"Didn't the Brazilian government recently have a team in here?" Laura asked and knew they had. She had a copy of the items they'd found and itemized. She also had a copy of the forensic reports on the bones of the porters they'd discovered.

It doesn't take the jungle long to reclaim what it considers its own." Jim observed and shed his backpack.

"So!" Kurt exclaimed, no more impressed than Laura. His gaze swept an area no less cluttered with greenery than any place else. For all he could tell, the carpet of creepers and vines could easily conceal another fissure. The adjoining pond was fairly large, made to seem smaller by the overhang of tree branches that threatened to close it off from two sides. It was backed by a basalt cliff that extended straight up and cut off even more light. At several spots along the cliff, water drooled, turned black stone more sinister, and entered the pool with nary a ripple. Atop the several-layered pile of lava were more trees, more vines, more bushes, more underbrush.

Kurt unloaded his pack and approached the pool. The liquid was clear along the shoreline nearest him, the glass-like water exposing volcanic rock that sprouted no green streamers to gently wave back and forth. A few yards out, there was a drop-off, and the water became opaque. Nearest the cliff, the water appeared downright milky.

"I need a bath," Laura said; Kurt turned as she joined him. "And, I mean to have one, even though it wasn't long ago I swore I'd never want to see water en masse again." She shrugged her shoulders, to relieve the stiffness brought on by lugging her backpack. "Tell me there's not some wretched pond creature waiting to suck me down."

"There's no wretched pond creature waiting to suck you down," Kurt obliged.

"Next time with real feeling, please!" she requested with a smile and linked her arm with his. She waited for revelation. What she received was the same inner sense of pleasure she always got when Kurt was near her, but that was all. She turned back over her shoulder toward Jim who had already used a stick to separate some greenery for whatever it might conceal. "Think this water is fit for bathing?" Laura asked him.

"Probably," Jim decided with enough gentlemanly interest to add: "Would you prefer we vacate the immediate premises to give you a little privacy?"

"Thanks, but I've given up bathing au naturel," Laura informed. Although she wasn't as verbal about it, she still carried with her that being-watched sense of ill-being. "I've shorts and a halter; so, you and Kurt should feel free to join me. Unless, of course, you'd prefer I vacate to give *you* guys some privacy?"

"Luckily, I brought swim trunks," Jim said.

"Kurt?" Laura asked and looked up at him.

"So did I," he grinned. "As a former boy scout I'm always prepared."

She knew she should be as eager as Jim to get started on their search, but the water beckoned, and she couldn't shake the feeling there was nothing new to be found here. It was almost as if the whole area had already turned itself upside down and emptied all its pockets: a street-wise con artist tickled pink at frustrating the police officers who frisked him.

"A bath sounds great," Kurt conceded, disappearing with Jim. Laura quickly changed into her shorts and halter. When she rejoined Kurt, she noticed the two large bruises on him, one on his left arm, one on his left thigh. They bore witness to the battering he'd taken on his mad sweep along the fissure. Laura, though, could match him bruise for bruise, and then some: one on her right shoulder, one on her left hip, one on her right forearm . . .

The water was pleasantly tepid and, at the shoreline surprisingly clear of silt or slime; hard granite refused to erode and let any quick-to-decay plants take root, and any dead leaves that had fallen from the parenthesizing trees had apparently settled out in the deeper, thoroughly uninviting water nearest the cliff.

Laura soaped herself and her clothing. What's more, she was determined to wash the rest of her dirty laundry once she was settled in. She was sick and tired of looking and feeling like something the cat dragged in.

Kurt splashed her with water, and she splashed him in return. Soon their raucous horseplay evidently became too much of an invitation for Jim who entered the water in a shallow dive. When he came up for air, he bellowed, "That *does* feel good!" with a shake of his head that splattered small drops of liquid, some of which caught a rare bit of sunlight to refract a momentary rainbow. Disturbed macaws, until then roosting in the branches of the trees that grew high atop the cliff, loudly took wing.

Eventually, Laura looked at her waterlogged skin." I think I'm nearly a prune. Shall we get out and get dried?" "Not that there's such a thing as "dry" in our present environment," Kurt teased as he hefted himself out and reached down to give her a hand. "The transition of skin from wet to sweat happens without any apparent interim. Clothes don't fare much better; no matter how long the material is left in the sun, it remains limp and displeasingly moist," Jim added.

Still, Laura found damp, clean clothes preferable to damp, dirty ones. Apparently, so did Jim and Kurt who soon joined her in scrubbing long-neglected laundry.

Such fun and games, followed by home-grown chores, didn't leave much time for a thorough reconnoiter of the area that evening, but it left everyone fresh enough for business the next morning.

Laura awoke to dense mist still clinging to the water and the trees. Both Kurt and Jim were already up, and the smells they'd produced with powdered eggs and dehydrated potatoes were a joy to the senses, even if the reality didn't live up to the come-on.

After that, it was all uphill. Each new discovery of a discolored piece of plastic, or piece of aluminum tubing, elicited a disintegrating level of excitement.

By the time Laura used a stick to push back a blanket of vines to uncover the thigh-thick anaconda coiled covetously around three rusted, dented, and now-empty metal tanks, she was ready for a break. Not that she was one to get hysterical over a snake. If she were, she certainly wouldn't have honed her camping skills in the Arizona desert which boasted more than it's fair share. However, this one was larger than any Arizona-born-and-bred variety, and a grotesque bulge in its midsection recalled a nature show where Marty Stouffer, or maybe it was Marlin Perkins, gleefully narrated as just such a monster unhinged its lower jaw to swallow a guinea pig. Laura was sure there was a message there somewhere: snake swallows guinea pig; jungle swallows Peter Lexly, Karl Reiger, Daniel Kenner; jungle maybe-yet-to-swallow Jim, Kurt, and her.

She shuddered and bumped into Kurt when she made a quick turn. He'd noted her intense concentration and had come for a look. Laura took hold of his arm for balance and left her fingers on his forearm after her balance was regained.

"Those *the* fuel tanks?" Kurt asked, referring to an entry on the list of scrap the Brazilian investigators had chronicled during their run-through of the area. "I thought they I.D.'d only three."

"The fourth, in case you'd care to notice, is a snake," Laura provided.

"I do believe you're right," Kurt admitted with mock surprise. "You handled that like a pro."

"You want to see a screaming-Mimi floor show, wait until I run across a slug," she guaranteed. "One of those giant, slimy, and particularly revolting variety."

"Something?" Jim called from down in a crouch. "I've a nineteen-sixty-one U.S. quarter. Which says the Brazilian team's sweep wasn't a perfect one."

There were six U.S. pennies, plus Brazilian coins equivalent to two-U.S.-dollars-and-forty-nine-U.S. cents, on the Brazilian investigatory team's list of things located in the area. No quarters, though. No paper money; it wouldn't have survived the damp. There was the top of a fountain pen; apparently, no one told Laura's father about ink that expanded with the heat.

There was a rusted German Luger; an acid bath had been required to bring out the serial numbers to match those of a gun owned by Karl Reiger; had Karl left it behind to confuse the issue? There was a belt buckle from the back of which an acid bath had coaxed: "T   Da   om i   "; "(To Dad from Jim?)" some Brazilian lab technician had conjectured correctly in a scrawl across the list's adjoining left-hand margin.

"Over here, we have the three fuel tanks and a large snake," Laura said.

"Oh," Jim responded, obviously not impressed; Laura didn't blame him.

"I need a carbohydrate fix," Laura told Kurt. "Which is your cue to give me a strip of fruit leather, preferably your apricot."

"My favorite: apricot," Kurt said with a feigned reluctance. "If you were anyone else, I'd say no, or, at least, try to bargain you back to less-desirable strawberry."

"Then I'm glad I'm me," she said. Then, with a frown, "Or is it I?"

"Whatever, come on!" He led the way to his pack. "I suppose you gobbled up your apricot first thing," he said and knelt to ferret it out.

"Actually, I'm saving mine," she admitted.

He waved a coveted cellophane-wrapped piece of apricot fruit leather in front of her, then pulled it back when she reached for it. "Why are you hoarding yours?" he asked curiously, waved the fruit leather again and, this time, was purposely too slow to prevent her from claiming it.

"For a special occasion," she said and pretended to protect her newly-won prize while she unwrapped it.

Kurt plopped down and used his pack as a backrest; Laura nestled against his left side and draped his left arm around her waist. Seeing the sudden potential for locating no clues whatsoever to their fathers' fate, she suspected that whatever Kurt and she had now wouldn't likely survive life outside this hostile environment. If that meant she might save herself heartbreak by gradually withdrawing from Kurt, starting now, she simply couldn't. Not until she had to.

Kurt ripped the cellophane on his fruit leather and took a large bite; Laura nibbled less greedily on hers, determined to savor her successful raid on Kurt's stockpile of sweets.

"You think we're going to have anything to celebrate?" Kurt asked. He *felt* pessimistic. They'd come a long way on what? Dreams, mainly. Hope. A lot of dreams and hope. Now that he'd realized his feelings for Laura, and she was surrendering to her feelings for him, dreams and hope were all the more important.

"Sure we are," Laura promised and wished she could sound more convincing. She snuggled to a more comfortable fit, slowly finished off her remaining fruit leather, shut her eyes, and marveled at how contentment could be as simple as tart sweetness on her tongue and this man close to her. She would miss such moments and worried that doing without was fast becoming a foregone conclusion.

She indulged in a catnap; when she opened her eyes, she had the solution. Just as it had been there for the Brazilian investigatory team, and as it was there for Jim and Kurt.

She scrambled to her feet without preamble. "Jim!" she called. "Can you come over for a minute, please?"

"Give me a minute," she instructed and left him for her pack. She knelt down, scrounged around and found what she wanted. She headed back to Kurt and to Jim who'd joined him.

"What's up?" Jim asked. He had a twisted piece of rusted wire that might, at one time, have belonged to just about anything.

"One for you, one for me, one for Kurt," Laura said and

passed out her surprise.

"Fruit leather?" Jim asked curiously.

"*Apricot* fruit leather?" Kurt queried and held it up for a better look.

"To celebrate," Laura insisted and got everyone's full attention. She would have liked drawing out the suspense, but she was too excited. "I know where they went," she blurted out breathlessly. Then, just in case she wasn't privy to that longheld secret, after all, she amended, "at least, I think I've deciphered a pretty good clue."

"What?" The men looked at her expectantly as they chewed the leather.

"Let's check those tanks." She led them back to the tanks. "See if they say 'air' on them."

"You say, 'Air'? Not kerosene, Coleman fuel, white or naphtha gas?" Jim queried and bent beside the three tanks. The anaconda, so recently coiled there, had gone, probably no more happy to have seen Laura than she had been to see it. Jim rolled each tank, in turn, apparently in search of content markings; however, weathering had done complete erasures. "This is the Amazon Basin — you do know? — not Mt. Everest where our fathers contemplated breathing problems at twenty-nine thousand feet."

"Aqua-lungs — of a sort?" Kurt divined and reflexively turned to face the pond and the new possibilities it suddenly offered.

"I remember tanks, not unlike these, from a Christmas in Bermuda," Laura said, barely able to control her excitement.

"Jim?" Kurt pressed for another opinion. He told himself not to get too worked up over pure speculation. Wanting something desperately didn't make it happen.

"The Loraline Sea Caves are accessed by water," Jim said

and then stood. He, too, faced the pond. "Aren't they?"

Neither Laura nor Kurt had heard of them and couldn't say.

"I've never been there," Jim confessed. "There always were so many other fascinating places to see that didn't require me starting out wet to see them."

"Didn't the Brazilian team check the pond?" Laura remembered and wished she didn't have to poke holes in her own theory. On the other hand, she had to be reasonable.

"They reported having *dredged* the pool," Jim emphasized. "Did that include shipping in divers and diving gear to do a thorough job? I didn't read it that way. Even if they did, did they have the wherewithal to poke around in every pockmark submerged at the base of the cliff?"

"There were experienced spelunkers in the original search teams," Kurt reminded.

"No one located this campsite twenty-four years ago," Jim argued. "Even if they had, nothing in my father's files, possibly a precaution he'd made against prying eyes, indicated access by water; although, someone as smart as Laura, given the chance back then, might have seen the tanks and read the clues. As it is, all these years later, how many people really care? The Brazilian team? Something tells me they were quite content to write down, 'Fuel tanks: three,' and leave it at that."

Laura took hold of Kurt's arm and gave it a squeeze.

"I say we take a good look and see," Jim said. "And, if Laura doesn't mind my doing first-time honors on this one . . ."

Did he sense that, while she'd had no trouble wading out to her neck for a swim and a bath, her recent experiences in the water-filled cave left her less inclined to play Jacques Cousteau than she once might have? Were his own watery nightmares, born of his almost drowning in the mines at Tenasco, so far removed that he could mock them now? "Please, be my guest," she readily consented.

"Want me to give you an assist?" Kurt volunteered; although, since his own experiences with water, he was a little leery of the soupy concoction seeming to await him at the base of the cliff.

"Let's see what I can come up with first," Jim suggested, heading back to the camp where he removed his shirt and pants and put on his swim trunks. "It looks a little murky at that end, and I wouldn't want either of us bumping heads underwater."

He led them down to the pool and sat on a rock to remove his boots. "I should emphasize the importance of not getting carried away by mere possibilities," he precautioned. "Say the tanks were once filled with air. Say access to the caves is by an underwater entrance. Does that mean, then, that we end up saying a tank-count of three, out here, insinuates our fathers never made it in there?"

"Maybe these are reserve tanks," Kurt suggested. He wanted it, and he was prepared to find every conceivable argument to support it.

"Maybe," Jim replied noncommittally.

"Maybe they didn't need the tanks once they got here," Laura rationalized. "My father swam varsity in college."

"Dad swam, too," Kurt remembered. Was he a good swimmer, though? It was sometimes hard to remember what his father looked like, without Kurt having a photo in hand; memories of seemingly less importance had faded even faster.

"And mine once swam the Amazon at Kenalanus," Jim admitted and commenced a series of arm-limbering exercises that, like his earlier dive, hinted he was no stranger to the sport. "The river is two miles across at Kenalanus," he added, his comment seemingly absent of boasting. "Sizable current to boot."

He took up position on the same flat slab of basalt that had earlier launched him into the pool. He bent low from his waist, reached his arms out over the water, and, simultaneously, pushed off with his feet.

Laura watched his shallow dive slice the water and glide him through the shallows and into the deeper, darker water above the drop-off. They'd previously kept clear of the milkier water adjoining the cliff. It had looked uninviting, still did, and the swim to get to it had never really seemed worth the effort.

"Could be limestone particles in suspension," Kurt commented on the pale-white opacity of the water. "A layer, down there, somewhere, slowly eroding. How logical it sounds— now."

Jim reached the cliff face, treaded water, filled his lungs with additional air. As he jackknifed, his head went under and his feet came up. There was a splash as he completely disappeared.

Laura's arm wrapped Kurt's waist; his wrapped hers. They held each other and silently counted seconds: one-thousand-one, one-thousand-two . . .

Jim emerged at the count of one-thousand-thirty. He called something, but neither Laura nor Kurt could be sure what it was.

Jim disappeared again, and the whole scenario was repeated; although, this time their count was one-thousand-forty-seven.

"Did he say, "It's a dead-end'?" Laura asked, Jim's next time up.

Kurt shrugged. "The accoustics are lousy," he complained, "but, if it's a dead-end, why would he be diving again?"

Jim went down twice more and apparently saved his breath by making no further attempt at distance communication. Dead-end or not, it seemed obvious, at least to Laura, that the cave entrance, if there, wasn't any too easy to locate.

"Has he been down over a minute?" Kurt asked suddenly and interrupted Laura's chain of thought.

"Has he?" Laura responded noncommittally and checked her watch which was another survivor of her near miss in the flooded cave. Frankly, she'd not kept track, this time around.

"He's been down a-minute-thirty," Kurt said a few seconds later and pulled away from Laura, his eyes focused entirely on the far end of the pool.

"Maybe he found something?" Laura ventured, but, she suspected Kurt, like she, was contemplating: "What if something found him?"

Kurt tore off his shirt without bothering with its buttons, and Laura chilled with her remembrance of Kurt's guarantee there was no monster lurking in the deep. How, though, could he know for sure what was born and bred in those milky depths and existed there even now? An anaconda? The one who'd left the tanks and decided on the seeming privacy of the water, now resentful of another intrusion? A crocodile—or, was it alligator? Laura never got the two straight, nor which hemisphere—or, was it which continent?—each exclusively called its own. A caiman? "Caiman!" someone had shouted on her boat trip up the Tapaua. Laura had rushed to the railing to see nothing but splash-rings radiating in the water.

Kurt got both boots off without their usual quota of unlacing. He entered the water with his pants and his socks still on.

Laura's imagination was now going full tilt: "Piranha?" she speculated. "Oh, please, dear God, not piranha!"

She remembered with another nature film with camera shot underwater, the fish in a feeding frenzy as they dined on some poor animal that had merely tried to swim to the opposite shore.

She hoped she'd once read how piranha required running water.

Trying to prevent her mind from taking farther flights of fancy, she told herself: "So what if some people think there's a prehistoric monster in Loch Ness, or others think there's a living fossil in an African lake? There's not positive proof to support such claims, only grainy pictures, that could be anything."

She checked her watch. Jim down way too long! Even she knew that now that Kurt had reached the cliff; he dived, came up, dived, came up, dived . . .

Suddenly, *he* didn't come up. Laura's heart stopped, then beat loud and fast. While long minutes dragged on: one, then two . . .

What to do? Go after him! It was inconceivable for Laura to stay put and hope for the best.

One boot off, she resented her uncoordinated fingers that refused to unfasten her other laces fast enough. "How had Kurt managed so fast?" she asked aloud, and water erupted from the pool, someone with it.

"Kurt?"

Blond hair: Jim! Alive and hopefully well. Waving. Shouting something—but what?

"Kurt went down after you!" Laura shouted back; he answered, but she couldn't hear him. "Kurt went down after you!" she repeated.

One boot on, one boot off, a clodhopper Cinderella, she splashed into the water, tripped and went down. Her knees contacted hard rock little cushioned by the water. Her spine telescoped, and her teeth rammed together with a force that hurt her jaw. Still, she was able to cast all of her discomfort aside, because she knew Kurt might need help, and she wanted Jim to help him. While it was rational that Jim alive, after so long underwater, meant Kurt had an equal chance for survival, she wasn't won over by that. In this place, under these circumstances, she'd be satisfied with nothing but ironclad guarantees.

She struggled back to her feet, slipped again, went down, but finally succeeded as Jim reached her.

He stood in the shallows, and water drained over his chest. A branch somewhere shifted, and sunlight was momentarily released to convert beaded moisture to countless reflecting crystals. Sunlight *did* so seem to love him!

"Kurt went down—" she began again.

"I know!" he interrupted and grabbed her in a wet embrace that took her breath away. "He's inside!" he announced cryptically, then elucidated: "I'm not just sure 'inside' what, but something *is* there; just like you said it would be."

"Kurt's okay?" she pressed. Whatever had been found down there, it would be, without Kurt, far less than Laura wanted—far less than she needed.

"He's fine," Jim insisted; Laura, weak-kneed, held on to him for support. His arm was rock solid beneath her gripping fingers; but she wished it were Kurt's water-beaded flesh. "He's catching his breath," Jim continued. "Quite a little chore getting in, let me tell you. Poor visibility all the way. Small hole. Narrow passage; too narrow for a man *and* an air tank, by the way. If our fathers used the tanks, it was only to reconnoiter the pool." Laura gave silent thanks for that explanation for the tanks left outside. "Part of the access tunnel heads down, just when you want air so badly that you're praying for it to go up," Jim hurried on. "Another part almost doubles back on itself. Then, once inside the cave, it's so dark I couldn't see my hand in front of my face. Shortly, thereafter, Kurt showed up with a splash and a gasp that scared the you-know-what out of me. I had to dive four times to find the way back out. Then, once en route, I got this horrible feeling I'd picked the wrong exit hole in the dark: one that would dead-end at any minute."

"You're *sure* Kurt is all right?" she persisted and knew she must sound like someone with a one-track mind. Nonetheless, she wanted additional assurances.

"Aside from breathless and in need of a flashlight, he's

fine," Jim assured and seemed blessedly uncritical of her redundant interrogation.

"I'm going in," Laura said. There was no other way. On the other hand, even though she'd reflexively been prepared to risk the trauma when she thought Kurt in danger, she didn't look forward to a replay of her lungs crying out for oxygen, while she imagined herself caught forever in a water grave.

"There *is* that old bit about getting back on the horse that's thrown you," Jim said. He was on her wavelength, just as he had been when he'd volunteered to explore her theory about the existence of the cave.

"I'll be fine."

"I've no doubt," Jim agreed, as if asked for a second opinion. "I'll just suggest that you make your attempt minus *both* boots."

Her one booted foot was magnified by the water she stood in. She couldn't help laughing at the absurdity. "Right!" she promised and let him help her out of the shallows.

She had trouble with soaked bootlaces. She did manage to shed her last boot while Jim secured two Tekna Xena Lites in a waterproof bag. "These lights are supposed to be waterproof to two-hundred feet," he said, "but I figure the EWA Water Safe Storage Bag is our second guarantee. Why don't you swim them in while I 'tree' our gear out here? I'd hate some animal to ransack our provisions while we're occupied. Not at this breakthrough juncture of our trip."

"Would you rather I stayed and helped?" She was torn two ways: not wanting to challenge the water; wanting to make sure the cave complex was there, Kurt safely in it.

"You go on," Jim insisted; Laura knew that was what she really wanted. "I promised Kurt that I'd send you in with a light, and I wouldn't want to disappoint either of you."

They walked to the edge of the pool, and he pointed toward

the cliff face. "There, where the shadows on the rock look like an elephant?" he directed. Immediately, Laura recognized the spot on the opposite wall of rock that was nearest to where Jim had last reappeared and where Kurt had made his recent heart-stopping dive.

Laura nodded that she saw the guide mark.

"Good!" Jim encouraged. "The hole you want is submerged right below it. Not the first hole you'll find on the way down, mind you," he warned. "that one only goes into the cliff about three yards. So, bypass it to where there's a slight bulge in the basalt; the hole you want is just underneath. It's not big, remember: maybe three feet in circumference. Venture off to the left or right, and there are other holes, some of which I checked out and found go nowhere."

"Got it!" Laura assured and tried to muster confidence to go with her words.

"If you can, do it by feel," Jim suggested. "The water irritates the eyes; there's a lot of fine particles suspended in it. Truth is, you can't see much with your eyes open, anyway."

Laura took a deep breath: one of many before the plunge.

"It gets a bit cramped in spots but *is* passable," Jim assured. "The walls seem pretty smooth: no jagged edges to get hung up on."

"Ready," Laura said but really meant: "Ready as I'm likely ever to be." Then again: "Possibly I should wear a bit less?" she stalled.

"Actually, I'm adding clothes for my next swim through," Jim argued. "Clothes, even damp, offer more insulation than wet skin. In fact, maybe you should take Kurt in a shirt." He nodded toward their full clothesline.

"Right!" Laura agreed, and, a few minutes later, the sleeves of Kurt's shirt were tied securely around her waist, much like she used to wear temporarily unneeded sweaters in high school and college. The flashlights were in a bag secured by a cord around her neck.

"You can move faster inside the tunnel if you use your hands to pull you along," Jim gave as a final point as he saw her into the water.

"Thanks," Laura said and, shortly thereafter, began her swim.

She knew, without looking, the minute she crossed over the drop-off. The water got no cooler, but there was a sense of wide-open spaces lurking in the depths below. After the drop-off, there was no seeing bottom, and the clarity got worse as the water turned milky.

The elephant shadow, close up, was distorted: more like a bulldog owned by a guy Laura once dated in Phoenix.

She treaded water, her legs straight down, and she remembered the printed promo for "Jaws" where a great-white shark, mouth agape, headed up from the deep to claim its unsuspecting victim forever suspended in water directly overhead.

She angled to face back toward shore. It was hard to see Jim from so low a vantage point, but she complied when he directed her more to her right and gave her the thumb's-up signal.

Without any more thoughts on the difficulty of the chore ahead, Laura put her right side toward the cliff and took three large breaths. Battling the additional buoyancy of the air she held in her lungs, she curled over, reached for the bottom, wherever it might be. Her feet momentarily kicked free of the water, then followed her into the deep.

Her shut eyes added to her claustrophobia, as did the heavy and clinging water that engulfed her. She dragged her right hand along the submerged cliff face and, when the basalt caved inward, like a toothless mouth, she lost contact until she was five seconds nearer the bottom of the pool.

This shrouding water wasn't in disconcerting motion. It

wasn't bashing her, like fists to her belly. It didn't turn her topsy-turvy, so she couldn't tell which way was up. In that sense, it was more docile than the water she'd battled in the cave off the fissure. In another sense, though, it had a malevolence all its own: a fake passivity.

When she found the hole, right where Jim said, she was sure it was the wrong one. Unlike a tooth cavity that could seem cavernous when checked by a nerve-rich tongue, this, explored by both hands, would have made a guppy feel closed in.

Appalled by the prospect of being swallowed alive by so small a throat, she didn't even risk a partial entry. She headed for the surface, stunned by how Jim and Kurt had accepted and succeeded in such a challenge.

Air suddenly seemed an eternity away. En route to it, she envisioned swimming in the wrong direction, destined to impact the bottom as her oxygen-deprived heart beat its last.

Finally, freedom! She tried unsuccessfully to make her air-starved gasp soundless. Simultaneously, she pictured Jim, his attention drawn by the noise as he confirmed his unspoken suspicions that she was too afraid to make a successful effort.

Sure enough, he was there. She gave him an everything-is-just-fine, that-was-just-a-trial-run wave of her hand. She took several large breaths, upturned her body once again, and retraced her way back down the cliff wall.

It wasn't a sudden absence of fear that spurred her on. It was her sense of do this or be denied whatever the firsthand revelations made possible by what was accessed only somewhere below her. If she didn't go forward—or, in this case, downward—she'd be left behind while Jim and Kurt went on without her.

So, if Jim could cover this route, after what he'd experienced in the mines at Tenasco, and, if Kurt could combat his fears that remained from his mad rush along the fissure, Laura surely had an equal reserve of nerve to put her fears at bay.

She swam past the nine-foot deep indentation that went nowhere. She reached the smaller hole beneath the bulge of basalt. She went into the seemingly miniscule opening and used her hands to pull herself deeper . . . deeper . . .

The passageway narrowed: rough stones against her shoulder: Jim said it was a tight squeeze. The tunnel looped right: Jim said it doubled back. It slanted downward: Jim said it went down when lungs begged it to go up.

Everything Jim had said made it easier: Laura would hate making the trip cold; but, it didn't make it easy enough! As the passageway continued, no sign of an underground complex, let alone breathable air, Laura's barely-subdued panic took control and demanded she turn back. It took a conscious effort to argue: she'd already probably consumed too much air to make it out the way she'd come in; besides, Jim would be disappointed; Kurt would wonder where she was; she would be delegated to guarding supplies while . . .

Quite suddenly, her head broke free of the all-confining water and took her so much by surprise that she was afraid to take a breath for fear she'd suck liquid.

"Laura?"

She opened her eyes to a darkness seemingly more complete than that found behind her closed lids.

"Kurt?" she queried and allowed herself a badly needed breath.

"Laura, over here!"

It *was* Kurt, and, shortly, his arms slid beneath her arms and lifted her onto a rock shelf.

Laura's weak legs, tired from their kicks to propel her to her destination, collapsed and she fell against him. Her arms slid up his arms and locked around his neck. The flashlights, still in their waterproof bag, hurt her as they became caught between the embracing bodies; the pain didn't matter: another affirmation she was here, Kurt was here, the cave was here, despite all odds against it.

"Oh, Kurt!" she exclaimed, raised on tiptoes, and counted on sixth sense, which didn't fail her, to put her lips to his.

A further continuance of the kiss took even more of her breath away.

"Is it really you?" he asked and sounded as breathless as Laura felt.

He hadn't been certain she'd come. Kurt's own fears had been conquered without thinking. He'd only known Jim had disappeared and was possibly in trouble; pure instinct had done the rest. For Laura, there'd been no distracting spontaneity. She'd faced her demons head-on and won out against them. Kurt envied her her strength. He did more than envy her, though. He was more sure each day that he loved her.

"What took you so long?" he asked and extended her to arm's-length. He preferred her closer, preferred more embraces, more kisses, but, because he loved her, he recognized the dangers in a darkness that falsely promised that no one, not even they, would see what they were about.

Heavenly Father saw!

Even if Laura's needs were the same as Kurt's, and he could only hope they were, it was up to him to do his part to keep them from going too far. What he wanted was right for Laura and him only after their marriage, and marriage wasn't possible if this underwater cavern was as much a dead-end as the one in the fissure. Which it might well turn out to be; up until now, its complete darkness had made anything but a superfical exploration impossible.

Even if this were one cave of the whole complex that their fathers had come to find and explore, evidence was needed of three dead men in here, evidence that could be laid before

Laura's mother as proof irrefutable that Karl Reiger hadn't maliciously, and with intent, disposed of his two friends in order to escape prosecution and punishment for crimes committed in World War II.

For Kurt and Laura to fool themselves into thinking they needed anything less, or would settle for anything less than what they deserved, would be a compromise of morals, principles, and beliefs: not worth a passing moment of pleasure stolen in the dark; at least, that was the way he saw it, and he was confident that Laura thought the same.

"I got here as quickly as I could," Laura managed finally. Had he felt the rapid beat of her heart, as she'd felt his? She was grateful he hadn't taken advantage of a situation that might have proved disastrous for both of them.

"Lady, do you have a light?" Kurt asked. "I could sure use one."

"Yes, a light," she agreed. "Actually, I've two Tekna . . ." She couldn't remember their names.

"Tekna Xena Lites," Kurt filled in for her. "Meaning, you've funny-looking flashlights, spotlights really, with xenon gas bulbs."

"In a waterproof bag around my neck," she completed.

"Ah-ha!" he exclaimed. "And, I have the bruises on my chest to prove it!"

"Don't feel like the Lone Ranger," she said, because she, too, had been subjected to the same discomfort of the package squeezed between them when they'd embraced so intently.

She left the bag around her neck while she tried to open it. What should have been no big deal—she'd opened countless such Ziploc bags to store leftovers—was hampered by nervous fingers she couldn't control.

"Success!" she proclaimed finally, surprised Kurt hadn't commented on the delay.

The Lites were more like small headlamps, suspended beneath one end of short handles, than they were like conventional flashlights. Holding one was like holding a frying pan, its switch on top where the handle connected; the light hung below. The switch was pressed by a thumb.

The two beams of resulting light blinded Laura after the completeness of the preceding darkness.

Only after some discomfort did she see what her Tekna's beam of light was illuminating as it crossed with Kurt's Tekna beam there in the cavern.

"Please, no?" she protested and felt desperately sick to her stomach.

7

"I know what you're thinking," Kurt accused; not that he blam-ed her. How many alternatives were there, after all, to explain three swastikas on the cave wall? "You think two victims of my ex-Nazi father found themselves in here, possibly wounded and dying, with no way out, and chose this particularly pictorial manner in which to disclose their fate to any future visitors."

If he didn't blame her, he did recognize how something as easily misinterpreted as this pointed out the tenuousness of their relationship, as long as his father's tainted reputation always hung over them. As he saw it, Laura continually teetered on a very narrow fence; her mother pulled from one side, and Kurt pulled from the other. Certain things, like three swastikas painted in a subterranean cave, had the potential for tipping the balance. He could tell, just by looking, that her mind played a mistakenly violent scenario. If he could successfully argue his case on this one, how would he fare further up the line if he didn't have as easily available answers?

Now, he had to re-inforce his arguments with more artistic inscriptions, ones less sinister and more seemingly indicative of a jungle locale; his light scanned the adjoining wall and stopped on the scrawled representation of a monkey. Below the monkey were three snakes drawn in an intricate entwining. "Did Jim's or your dying father draw those, too, I wonder?" he asked and tried to keep out any sarcasm.

Frankly, Laura didn't know what to think. Here, years and miles away from Nazi Germany, in a cavern in the middle of the Amazon Basin, she'd been startled by swastikas on the cave wall. Monkeys and snakes there, too, didn't change that.

"Among other things, Hitler was a thief," Kurt said and shifted his voice into emotionless neutral; he didn't like the sound: it reminded him too much of Marc Klexter. "Hitler didn't sit down one fine day and conceive the swastika, as an original thought, from his pea brain, as *the* insignia to represent his band of butchers. He lifted it from— Take your pick: the Persians, the Trojans, the Chinese, the Japanese, the Koreans, even the native Brazilians. All of those peoples employed the swastika, fylfot, or 'four-foot' cross, as a sign of good luck, or as a symbol of welfare. The Buddhists painted it on their shrines centuries before Hitler put it against a black-white-red background and hoisted it high above his *Nationalsozialistische Deutsche Arbeiterpartei.*"

Recognizing and regretting the residue of tension this incident left between them, Laura silently accompanied Kurt in a once-over of the cavern.

Laura felt a little ridiculous, because she wasn't illiterate, after all, and she had read more than her share of books on Germany. Anyway, her father's possible murder by a Nazi war criminal had given her more incentive to look into German politics, of the late thirties and into the forties, than the average woman on the street. So, how had she let all of the swastika trivia run off her back like water, retaining only the more sinister connotations? How much better it would have been if she'd not been shocked at all by what she'd seen, but had been able to calmly spout off swastika genealogy to Kurt. Unfortunately, she *had* thought the worst, and that painfully illustrated just how tentative were the foundations upon which Kurt and she hoped to build something permanent.

They found two more things of interest: an obviously old statuette and a tunnel. Jim arrived and proved himself another font of information on the subject of swastikas: "Kurt is quite right. Hitler wanted a flag to compete with the glaring red of the Communist banner: 'Something red enough to out-Herod Herod!' was how one of his cronies put it. Jim continued: "Actually, swastika is Sanskrit for 'all is all' — long a slogan of the Teutonic Knights. It goes back farther than that, though. There's record of it used in the Bronze Age among the ruins of prehistoric Swiss lake-dwellers. It's even been found in North and South America. So, what we have is an unfortunate coincidence, not as rare as one might originally suppose."

He gave Laura a sympathetic smile, as if he'd sensed the tension in the air and hoped he'd done something to diffuse it.

"Anything else of interest?" he asked and flashed a light farther along the wall. He stopped it briefly at the monkey and the snakes. "If nothing else comes of this little adventure, all of this will certainly raise curiosity among the world archaelogical community," he predicted. "Considering the moisture from water, so near, these pictures are surprisingly well-preserved. I wonder what they were painted with."

"A statuette of some kind is in a recess over there," Kurt moved on, and his light pinpointed the area in question.

"How interesting!" Jim exclaimed in appreciation. He walked over for a closer look. "Any ideas as to origin?" he asked and lifted the jaguar-headed image off its terra-cotta base. "Certainly nothing I've ever seen indicative to this area. Almost Egyptian, isn't it? And, what's it carved of? Serpentine? Jadite? Jade?"

"I have no idea," Laura said.

"We've located a dry tunnel-to-somewhere, but only one."

"Ah!" Jim exclaimed, and his interest shifted away from the statuette which he quickly returned to its niche. "Have you reconnoitered at all?"

"We didn't think it wise to wander off and expect you to guess where we were." Laura informed, "but it was admittedly hard to resist that temptation."

"For your reward, I've brought in a stove, gas, some food, canteens, guns, and, for each of us, boots and a dry change of clothing," he said and nodded toward the waterproof stuff bag he'd ferried in with him. "At least, the clothing is as dry as the outside conditions ever allowed it to be. Speaking of outside, I left a note detailing our whereabouts for Captain Fortuna-Mata—just in case." He didn't have to specify that his precaution was one to prevent their disappearances, without a trace, as their fathers had done before them.

They showed him the dry tunnel.

"Certainly more commodious than our entranceway," Kurt pointed out; the tunnel swallowed all light and returned none of it. "Looks like a fairly straight run, at least for a few yards."

"So, I presume you both are as anxious as I am to get started," Jim said.

"Yes!" Kurt and Laura chorused.

"Well, let's change into drier clothes and have something to eat," Jim said.

"Good idea." Kurt replied. It makes sense to start our exploration with a full stomach."

The hot meal was Turkey Tetrazzini which might have been "Cardboard Tetrazzini" for all its similarity to the real thing.

When they finished the meal, Jim said, "We'll reconnoiter far enough to make sure it's worth our while to ferry in additional supplies from our outside stockpile. We wouldn't want to waste time, effort and breath to move in most of our stuff if the tunnel peters out around its first bend.

"We'll have to leave ourselves plenty of energy to make it back here and out for this evening," he added, and took another bite of pemmican. "I don't look forward to going back-and-forth through that watery tunnel," Laura said. "Of course, we could sack out somewhere in here for tonight, but there's no point in making ourselves uncomfortable when our bedding is outside; fatigue isn't something we want to encourage in circumstances like these, that may require fast reflexes for self-preservation." Kurt said.

"It's debatable which is the more fatiguing: the loss of a good-night's sleep, or the long swim out, then *back again* in the morning." Laura argued.

Jim continued: "If what we find, during these next couple of hours, shows potential for a more concentrated effort, we'll cram our bedding in waterproof stuff bags and bring it in with whatever else we need. Our supplies, food included, are pretty much packaged in the waterproof bags we used in anticipation of the rainfall above ground. Our backpacks can be broken down into manageable aluminum tubing and easily folded canvas. Whether or not our caving gear gets wet is inconsequential."

He finished his trail bar, and Laura did the same with hers. Kurt, who'd skipped dessert, got to his feet. "I presume we'll take with us all we do have on hand," he said.

Jim had brought in enough food for several days, and the group only planned to reconnoiter a few hours, but no one knew what existed just up the way to delay them. "Always best to have too much food, rather than not enough," he said, and disconnected the one-liter aluminum fuel bottle from the stove. The thin aluminum reflector easily folded; the stove's three wire legs collasped; altogether, it formed a very small and lightweight package.

"We certainly have it more convenient than our fathers," Laura commented. "At least our basic camping equipment has become miniaturized."

Everything back into the stuff bag Jim had used to bring it in, Kurt took first duty as pack horse, and the three headed off to see what the tunnel had in store for them.

The passageway turned out to be quite straightforward, with no successful booby traps. Its curved ceiling and walls were smooth as a man-made culvert and, like the fissure, gave the impression of massive natural scouring; Laura, more familiar with cave environments, suspected the last of the carving had been completed thousands, even millions of years before; but, nevertheless, she kept her ears open. Her close call in the fissure had left her far less trusting.

There were no branch tunnels to confuse, no sudden chasms in the floor, no uncomfortable constriction of the passage so the group made excellent time.

There were several aneurysmal bulges of the tunnel: room-like appendages, fairly small, that resembled empty garages or vacant storage areas. After which, there was a cavern that finally lived up to all the stereotypical expectations of anyone whose only exposure to spelunking was compliments of *National Geographic* or *Natural History Magazine*.

"Now, this is more like it!" Laura admitted. Her spelunker's enthusiasm was tempered only by no evidence that their fathers had been this way before them. For that matter, beyond the petroglyphs and statuette of the first cave, nothing indicated Indians — recent or long-past — had been this way, either.

"Certainly is pretty," Kurt agreed and watched the reflection of their lights off pure-white calcareous incrustations. "In a cold, otherworldly sort of way."

Like predators' teeth, stalactites drooled from the ceiling. More teeth, this time stalagmites, but upward from the floor. Sometimes, two opposing formations met and formed a pillar: columns and caryatids that seemingly supported the weight of the ceiling. From an ancient crack in the roof had oozed, one thin line at a time, a sheet of satiny dripstone which now hung like a breeze-disturbed curtain. A similar flowstone formation coated one wall in a tapestry-like design.

There were two exits, besides the one through which they'd entered. The group chose the one accessed between the flowstone and dripstone. The tunnel, large enough to allow them to walk upright, led, in a very short time, to an impassable rock wall.

They backtracked without much effort and took the second tunnel which required progression in humpbacked fashion. Even then, the going was surprisingly easy, and they were rewarded for even those efforts by another underground cavern more striking than the one they'd just left.

Their lights crisscrossed the interior, and Laura was struck by how imperfections in rock, this time in the form of contaminating chemicals coloring the limestone, were like physical imperfections in people: they could make *some* beauty far more approachable. The dripstones here, every one, were polluted by extravagances of color: rich greens, warm reds, shiny blues, velvety pinks, deep oranges . . .

Apparently less bowled over than Laura by the sheer technicolor, Jim used his light to pinpoint two exits from the room. Without much additional effort, he quickly located two more. "Although none possibly lead anywhere," Jim admitted, "I suspect they're incentive enough for us to bring in a bit more of our gear for an extended siege."

"I'll agree to that," Laura conceded. "Kurt?"

"By all means," Kurt said.

"Then, I suggest we take a short break, now, and head back to organize a more concentrated plan of attack," Jim recommended.

However, while all agreed to the break, none took real advantage of it.

For Laura, the subterranean room was a true treasure to be further explored and enjoyed. She felt as if she'd stepped inside the crystalline interior of a giant geode not yet cleaved for display in some hobby shop. The colors were quite wonderful; she couldn't remember such a dazzling display, not even the renowned west Texas Coorelling Spring Caves that were, each in its own right, a perfect little jewel.

She wandered along the curve of one wall, careful to keep oriented. If the cavern wasn't massive, Jim and Kurt's lights enough to keep the two men accurately pinpointed from most parts of the room, it was large enough and dark enough so that, more than once, a looming limestone column isolated Laura with only her light for reassurance and comfort.

It was an unexpected heap of rough and irregular stone pieces, piled high against the symmetry and smoothness of the adjoining stone, that caught Laura's attention. The colors of the broken rock remained intact but seemed as fragmented as the haphazard arrangement of the limestone chunks that contained them: a collage formed by a cave-in.

The resulting hodgepodge reminded Laura that danger could lurk even among all of this loveliness. At any moment, a colored stalactite, weakened structurally by a recent, or long-ago earthquake. or by faulty layering, or by sheer weight built into it over the centuries, could break off and kill her. A thin layer of flowstone, once liquid, now solidified atop a limestone floor long since eroded into a deep hole, could open at the slightest pressure of her misplaced foot. On her walk out, she could become the victim of a tunnel collapse.

Laura yearned for a world wherein there were at least temporary respites from life-threatening situations. Since she'd reached Brazil, it was one danger after another; they eroded her nerves as surely as water had eroded stone to make this cavern. Still, she would subject herself to even more of the same, because the rewards in successfully meeting the challenge, and succeeding in it, opened up so many more possibilities for her than she'd originally imagined possible.

It was a seemingly innocuous bit of drabness that brought Laura out of her reverie by its refusal to blend in with the color that surrounded it.

Laura knelt and looped her finger around a dull-colored chain; her heart skipped a beat. She gave a tug, and more of the chain came free; loose rock slid with it, riding atop the metal of a flattened canteen.

"Here!" she shouted, finally finding the voice she'd swallowed. Simultaneously, she cleared away the hitchhiker stones, and, in the process, disturbed nearby bits of rock to reveal mummified fingers and a bright gold wedding band; the combination made her feel faint and dizzy. "Here!" she repeated weakly and pushed back into a crouch.

She crossed her arms in an unsuccessful effort to control the massive shudder that took hold and shook her with a force that chattered her teeth.

"Daddy?" she moaned and started to cry.

Kurt and Jim hurried over.

Laura pointed to what she'd found and they knelt and started clearing away the rest of the rocks.

Still chilled, Laura sat off to one side. Kurt joined her.

" 'To P. —lovingly— J.,' " he recited the inscription from inside the gold band he turned over to her. "You recognized the ring?"

"Maybe," she hesitated; the gold was cool in her hand, and she tried it on. It was too big; she didn't remember her father's hands so large. "It was more intuition," she admitted. "That psychic something Jim always predicted from the three of us."

"How do you feel?" he asked and gave her a hug.

"Grief; relief," she said. "If that's a paradox, so be it! I'm sorry he's dead, but it gives a welcome and long-overdue finality. You know what else I feel?" Her question was rhetorical. "Sadness that it wasn't your father, because it's he that you and I have to find here."

She was still cold, but his warmth made it bearable.

"Thank you for that," he said and kissed her forehead.

She leaned against him, her head on his shoulder, her hand in his.

"There's the chance all three were buried in the cave-in," Kurt said.

"I'll help you," Laura insisted. She heard Jim working. "First, though . . ." She took a handkerchief from a pocket and wrapped her father's ring inside.

"Some of the rocks are large and heavy," he said, prepared to give her an out. A woman who'd just stumbled upon the remains of her father might be excused from digging for two more dead men.

"So, I'll lift smaller, lighter ones," she countered.

Her father found solved one mystery, but that was no longer enough; Laura's happiness depended upon finding Karl Reiger. Her mother would read this evidence as: "An engineered cave-in. What better than a ton of rocks to conceal his crime?"

"We *have* to find your father," Laura insisted. "There's no other way for us, is there?"

"Another one!" Jim called from among lights angled to aid in his clearing the rubble.

Kurt and Laura moved quickly, Laura relieved the two men had once again concealed her father; people more expert in such things would be brought in to transfer the remains back to the States.

Laura watched Kurt help Jim move one of the large chunks of rock that concealed most of the latest discovery.

Laura, who'd expected stark skeletons, was again surprised by something more akin to a mummy seen in the Cairo Museum. Here, no wild animals had desecrated or scattered remains. Here, no sun had bleached bones. Here, temperatures, cooler than the heated humidity above ground, had been kind.

Laura helped with the smaller stones, anxious for an identification. She was consoled in her chore by her self-assurances that their intentions were honorable and loving; they weren't robbers out to plunder graves.

"My father's I.D. bracelet!"

And who said that? Kurt? Laura hoped, with all her heart, that it was Kurt, but it was Jim who retrieved the platinum wristband. Laura was pleased for Jim— She knew the burden relieved by a father found—but was disappointed, too.

"We'll keep searching," Jim said, after a few minutes of silence over his father. He sounded convinced that Karl Reiger was only a few piled stones away; Laura wasn't nearly as confident.

As with Laura's father, they carefully reconcealed Daniel Kenner before they moved on to further clearing.

If Laura held out hope that Karl Reiger would be revealed beneath each newly excavated chunk of limestone, she was continually disappointed. There was only more stone beneath more stone.

"No one said they were linked like Siamese triplets when the disaster struck," Jim optimistically reminded them and relayed another fragment to Kurt who tossed it; the bracelet on Jim's wrist caught the light and reminded that the expedition was two-thirds successful.

They no longer talked of a return to the outside in order to plan a more full-scale operation, nor of a good-night's rest. They had food; discomfort and sleeplessness were acceptable under these revised circumstances.

Whenever one of them got tired, he moved off to one side, either for a rest or a catnap. Anyone with the energy pressed on. Laura now knew why prisoners were so often relegated to rock piles; the work exhausted, left no energy for small talk, and seemed never-ending.

Kurt reached for a rock halfway up the receding pile. Under its own weight, it fell away before Kurt took hold, and it left a hole soon filled by a cascade of smaller stones from farther up the pile. Then, like a stack of cards, the whole pile collapsed of its own volition.

"Back!" Kurt warned and bodily took Laura out of the way.

Jim, who'd been napping until spurred into action by automatic reflexes, showed his sleepy disorientation with: "What's happened?"

"What got our fathers tried to get us, too," Kurt replied.

He was wrong, though; the last of the barricade had simply collapsed to reveal, "Another avenue out?" Jim ventured.

"You two wait here," Kurt instructed. "I'll check it out."

"Why don't you wait until more dust settles?" Laura suggested and held tightly to him in emphasis. "If the ceiling collapsed once, more of it could collapse, even all of these years later."

"I'll be fine," he promised; but Laura didn't see how he could make good any such promise. They were dealing with nature, and nature didn't honor the assurances of a man. On the other hand, Laura knew he had to go, if just because his father's whereabouts were still in question. If Karl Reiger wasn't beneath the rocks of the cave-in, then where? Someplace in South America?

"I'll be okay, Laura, really," Kurt insisted and tried to read the expression on her face. Her concern was obvious, but what else was there? He knew what he'd think if he were she, Peter Lexly and Daniel Kenner found but Karl Reiger still missing.

"I'll hold you to that," Laura said and reluctantly turned him loose. As soon as he was gone, she asked herself silently what everyone wanted to know: *Where is Karl Reiger?*

Shortly, Kurt brought her the answer: "Dad's just on the other side," he said. Kurt had his dad's ring to prove it: gold with a star sapphire whose identifying asterisk was evident even in the dim lighting.

"Oh, Kurt!" Laura exclaimed; he accepted her with open arms.

"Apparently, the cave-in missed him," Kurt said. "He held out long enough to clear away a lot of the stone from his end, or we wouldn't have broken through nearly as fast."

Laura held him tighter and still couldn't believe this wondrous moment had come.

The sudden gunshots were something with which Laura was familiar. When Jim had written her that she'd need a revolver, Laura hadn't just gone down, picked one up, and left it at that. She'd gone, three nights a week, for four weeks, to Klyndale Firing and Archery Range outside Phoenix—to learn firing and gun safety. Ear plugs worn at the time, or not, Laura knew the sound of a bullet. However, like the roaring water in the fissure, a sound with which she'd been familiar from her childhood experiences in the caves at Mesa Juanita, her identifying these sounds was slow in coming, because, they, too, seemed so out of context. Also, Laura was confused by the way Jim lurched backward and collided against the cavern wall while, simultaneously, Laura was splattered by splinter-like pieces of rock exploded off a nearby column of stone.

Her first impression was of a stalactite broke off at its base and crashed to the floor. Thank goodness, her automatic response to Kurt's, "Douse the lights!" was quicker. She dived for one light and wrestled it off; Kurt did the same for another. Laura would have moved on to the remaining third light, but Kurt grabbed hold of her and pulled her into the protection of the recently excavated tunnel; all the while, there were more of the same sounds.

"Gunfire?" Laura asked; Kurt went down and Laura, confused, went down hard against him. He breathed erratically; her breaths were little gasps, and she experienced the light-headed buzz of adrenaline loose inside her.

"I'd say that's definitely gunfire!" Kurt concluded with unarguable finality.

"Are you okay?" she asked him, afraid he'd been wounded.

"I think so. You?"

"Yes, fine," she said; she didn't mention the sting from rock that had ricocheted off her arm.

"I don't think Jim was so lucky," Kurt prophesied.

Visions of Jim, slammed against the cavern wall, flashed through Laura's brain. "Ohhhh, no!" she groaned in response.

"You have your gun?" Kurt asked; his was drawn.

Laura unsnapped her holster and withdrew cold metal. Despite her experience at the firing range, she'd never considered any weapon, not even this one, user friendly.

"If anyone shines a light, open fire," Kurt instructed. He aimed his gun at the remaining light of theirs which, still on, had somehow become enlodged face up among the rocks. Kurt squeezed off the trigger of his gun, and the light went out with an accompanying explosion of plastic and xenon bulb.

Laura didn't see Kurt go, because she couldn't see anything, but, immediately upon his leaving, she felt his absence. Her impulse was to call after him, but she controlled herself; she didn't want the enemy to know Kurt was on the move.

That Kurt had gone after Jim was confirmed by an enemy's light that went on and quickly traveled the distance to Kurt who dragged an unconscious Jim in Laura's direction.

Without forethought, Laura shifted the aim of the pistol already extended by her locked arms in front of her and pulled the trigger. The resulting reverberation jolted her. It happened so fast, it was only the arrival of Kurt, Jim in tow, accompanied by Kurt's congratulatory, "Good girl!" that confirmed there was no light where there'd once been.

"Who's out there?" Laura asked, amazed that she sounded as if Kurt might know. If she'd been sure, from almost the beginning, that they were being followed, she couldn't put rhyme or reason to such violence now, except as an anathema to her possibilities for happiness with Kurt now that Karl Reiger was found.

"I figure thieves, for want of a better explanation," Kurt ventured.

"Thieves?" Laura echoed and tried to get her thoughts unjumbled.

"The ones who steal on-site archaelogical artifacts," Kurt elucidated. "Captain Fortuna-Mata mentioned them, remember? The ones who hack up whole buildings and cart them away for sale on the black market."

"Why would they want to kill us?" Laura asked. She knew it would all fit if she gave herself time. However, did she have time?

"They followed us in . . ."

"We keep saying, 'they,' don't we?" Laura interrupted.

"Better to expect the worst," Kurt argued. "Maybe, they—" This time Laura didn't interrupt. "—thought we were treasure hunters and would lead them to something; they followed us in

with no problem, because Jim conveniently left explicit instructions that told Captain Fortuna-Mata where he could find
us—if and when. Once in, they grabbed up the statuette, maybe
have designs on gouging the monkey, snakes, and swastika
petroglyphs out on the wall."

"Why kill us?" Laura asked, then she made her own guesses.
"Because it takes time to chisel off petroglyphs? Because what
they're doing is illegal, and why leave potential witnesses?"

"Elementary, my dear Watson."

"What do we do?" Laura asked and reached out for comfort
in the darkness.

Her hand squeezed his arm with a pressure that must have
relayed the extent of the cold fear racing through her, there in
the blackness, because he said: "First off, we don't lose our
cool."

"Right!" she agreed. Logic, as well as Kurt, told her she
would be of little use to him, or to Jim, once she went off the
deep end. And, after all, what was an ambush by thieves, considering everything else she'd been through?

"I suggest we retreat to a position where we can shine a little
light, figuratively and literally, on just how bad Jim is," Kurt
suggested. "All I can tell is that he's still alive." Laura, too,
could hear Jim's labored breathing.

"Retreat to where?" Laura whispered nervously, then realized they only had one real alternative. Luckily, the tunnel was
now cleared, or they would have had no easy route for
withdrawal.

"The tunnel branches on the other side of where we cleared
the cave-in," Kurt said. "If we take one tunnel, we can hope
they'll take the other."

"Works for me," Laura agreed; there was little point in a
pessimistic reminder that more than one thief meant the at-
tackers could split up. Besides, there was something encourag-

ing about, "Together we stand, divided *they* fall!"

"We'll need the stuff bag with our supplies," Kurt informed.

Laura felt new panic. She'd had time to realize how easily Kurt could have been the one wounded if the gun that shot Jim had been aimed a few inches in another direction. What's more, Kurt had already risked his life once when he'd gone back for Jim. If Laura understood that risk, she wasn't sure she could accept the one that put him in danger for a stuff bag.

"Even if we can't risk a lit stove, the trail bars will come in handy if we're pinned down for long," Kurt reminded.

"Do you even remember where the stuff bag is?" Laura asked, because the darkness hid all reference points.

"I think I can find it," Kurt assured, "but I need you to distract our visitors with a few shots. Ready?"

"Ready?" she said, and, as soon as she sensed him on the move, she fired two shots high into the darkness. She fired one more when Kurt made a noise that might have pinpointed him for an enemy bullet.

No shots were returned, and Laura hoped she'd hit something. However, her Rambo fantasy was short-lived.

"Leave Jim where he is, and we'll let the two of you go," a familiar voice crossed over to Laura.

"Marc Klexter?" Laura accused.

"Kurt?" Marc asked, apparently prepared to ignore Laura.

"What's this about?" Laura demanded.

"Kurt?" Marc repeated and whispered something that came to Laura undecipherable.

Two lights suddenly came on and swept the space in front of the tunnel. Unlike a frightened animal, mesmerized into inaction by exposure to a spotlight, Kurt was spurred to move faster now that he could see; he had the stuff bag beneath his arm. Simultaneously, Laura fired at one light, then the other, in quick succession.

She didn't realize when Kurt rejoined her until he touched her in renewed darkness.

"It's okay, Laura," he consoled and moved closer. His arms wrapped her trembling body, and she turned her head into his shoulder. Why, she wondered, was it always one thing after another? Karl located, this should have been a happy time for them; it had degenerated into another nightmare.

"It's Marc Klexter out there!" Laura informed. She spoke into the cloth of his shirt, and her free hand took a handful of the material; her other hand was still locked about the hardness of her now-empty gun.

"This is Marc Klexter!" Marc confirmed.

"What's this about, Klexter?" Kurt demanded. His artifact-thieves theory no longer seemed as likely, unless Marc and his band of botanists operated under a legitimate cover.

"You owe me, Kurt," Marc reminded. "I saved your life, remember? Now, all you have to do to clear that debt is leave Jim behind, take your girl friend, and scoot out of here to a happy-ever-after ending."

"Why do you suddenly want Jim?" Laura demanded.

"You have my word on a safe passage out of here, Kurt," Marc said; he'd ignored Laura's question. "Why not take advantage of it. You have what you came for, don't you? My congratulations, by the way, on a job well done."

"Why do you want Jim?" Laura repeated, not to be denied.

"I'd prefer if you didn't let a woman do your talking for you, Kurt," Marc berated. "This is man's business, and Laura is so . . . female-emotional."

"I always knew you were a male chauvinist!" Laura yelled. It probably accomplished little more than making her feel better, but that was enough, as far as she was concerned.

"You'll let Laura and me go?" Kurt ventured dubiously.

"We don't want either of you, I assure you," Marc cajoled. "You're still alive, aren't you?"

"I figured that's because one or more of you are lousy shots — under these less than ideal conditions," Kurt countered.

There was some obviously unhappy whispering in the darkness, but Marc's voice, when it returned to the conversation, was its same unemotional monotone. "It's just Jim we want," he reassured. "Is he dead, by the way? Not that it matters. Quite frankly, we'll take him any way we can get him."

"I wouldn't trust you any farther than I could throw the nearest ten ton stalagmite!" Laura informed him.

"Let us have a few minutes to think it over," Kurt stalled.

"Surely, there's nothing to think over!" Laura protested. "That man, or one of his sleazy cohorts, gunned Jim down without warning."

"Just remember that the sooner you decide to leave, the sooner you can resume life in a more civilized and less dangerous environment.

"Well, *my* decision is made," Laura informed loudly. "Marc can take his offer and stuff it!"

"Your decision, Laura, doesn't much count in a world of men, does it, Kurt?" Marc mocked.

"I said we'd think it over," Kurt said; and, Laura couldn't believe he was serious.

He wasn't: "Take this," he whispered to Laura and handed her the stuff bag. "It, you, Jim and I are getting out of here!"

Kurt carried Jim like he'd wear a cape; Jim's arms were wrapped forward around Kurt's neck. Laura carried the stuff bag and her gun, the latter reloaded. Laura brought up the rear, her weapon aimed behind them. Every few steps, they stopped and listened, Laura prepared to fire at the least provocation.

Their progress was slow and none too silent, hindered by a carpet of stony fragments that wasn't easily maneuvered in the dark. More than once, Laura tripped and almost fell, positive her sounds would draw enemy fire.

Beyond the once-blocked area, the going was easier, although complete darkness remained a problem. Darkness above ground was something in which eyes eventually began to detect forms and shadows; not this darkness: no moon, no stars, no light source whatsoever: nothing revealed, not even a hand held right in front of a face.

"We've just put a bend between them and us," Kurt whispered and stopped. Laura bumped into him and wondered how he'd detected the bend when she hadn't; then, she remembered he'd been this far before. His father was here somewhere, and Laura shivered at the idea of finally meeting up with Karl Reiger in this darkness. "The branching is just uphead," Kurt continued. "For the moment though—" He lowered Jim and propped him against the wall. "—I want you two to stay here."

"While you go where and do what?" Laura interrogated and tried to sound calm, cool and collected. She'd never fancied herself alone in this place, and her phobia was on the increase.

"I want to fire a few shots back the way we've come," Kurt explained, "in case Marc and his friends are already moving in. With the bend for cover, I'll be less likely hit if they shoot back."

"Okay," Laura agreed. Anything to keep the enemy at bay was okay by her.

"And, Laura?" Kurt asked. He somehow found her, despite the darkness, and wrapped her in his strong arms. "Did I tell you how glad I am you're along as backup?"

"Tell me now," she cajoled while she savored the protection of his enfolding embrace.

"I'm glad you're along as backup," he obliged. He started at her forehead and kissed his way to her lips.

She balanced on her tiptoes and leaned against him. She

took renewed strength from his kiss.

"What *is* this all about?" she asked, their kiss reluctantly broken.

"It's called love," Kurt explained.

"I'm not talking obvious love in the dark, and you know it," Laura said, although she liked to hear him say it.

"Oh!" Kurt responded in mock surprise. "Well, as for *that*, 'What's going on?' we can only hope Jim's not too badly wounded and will soon regain consciousness long enough to tell us."

"You think he knows, then?" Laura asked and tried to remember any clue that Jim had previously known Marc, or vice versa. Frustratingly, she couldn't conjure a one.

"If he doesn't," Kurt said, "there's only Marc to fill in the blanks."

"When Marc had us all off guard, having saved you, he could have killed any of us easier than doing it here," Laura couldn't understand.

"I know," Kurt agreed; he didn't have the answers, either. So, he aimed a kiss for her lips and kissed the tip of her nose instead.

A few seconds later, he blasted five bullets down the corridor behind them; Laura could see each flash at the muzzle of his gun, and she reflexively recoiled at the sight and the sound of each of them. Seven shots were returned, and Laura recoiled at those, too; she could tell, by the sounds of bullet impacts, that Marc and his party were better situated for accessing the tunnel than they had been. She thanked her lucky stars that there was the bend between them.

"That should give them pause," Kurt predicted. So silent had been his return to Laura, it made her hope none of Marc's group was as cat-like; the thought not a pleasant one. "In the meantime," Kurt said, "we should put all the distance we can between us."

He talked her through the darkness and into one of the two branching tunnels. "If you can, drag your hand along the wall," he instructed. "It'll keep you oriented."

When they rounded the next bend, he surprised her with the light he'd brought with him after he'd turned it off back in the cavern. Laura wished she'd absconded with the light she'd switched off; but, she'd been so intent, at the time, upon moving on to disengage the third and last light, the one Kurt eventually blasted to smithereens, she'd not wanted herself encumbered with excess baggage.

They examined Jim: "Looks like a nasty shoulder wound," Kurt diagnosed; Laura agreed. "he probably was knocked out by his collision with the wall."

A bit of luck, in their favor, was the way the passageway shortly began a series of tight twists and turns that further promised to keep their light hidden from anyone following. The meandering continued until it opened suddenly into a subterranean room; Laura wasn't sure, though, they'd been done any favors, because she experienced a disquieting sensation that swept over her. Their light crossed a segment of seemingly empty landscape to be swallowed by ravenous blackness beyond. The air contained a suspension of lighter-than-air particles that made it as milky as the water they'd swum into the cavern system.

"All we need is a cave with a terminal case of dandruff," Laura whispered, all the while she concentrated on any signs of an enemy light coming up behind them.

"Do we move left, or right, and hug the wall?" Kurt offered. "Or—" He swept their light back and forth in front of them. "—do we tempt our luck out there: a lot of open space and darkness to hide in. Whatever, we're going to leave a trail," he regretted and kicked the thick inches of fine dust accumulated over the centuries on the floor.

"I vote for open spaces," Laura cast her ballot. Why not?: it sounded as if any choice would put them between the Devil and the deep-blue sea. In preparation, she wrapped her handkerchief around her nose and mouth; first, she made sure she'd unwrapped her father's ring and transferred it safely back into her pocket.

Kurt laid Jim down long enough to give them both the benefit of a kerchief face mask.

They moved out; as far as Kurt and Laura could tell, there were neither stalagmites nor stalactites. The few times Kurt aimed their light upward, there was no evidence of any kind of roof.

What they eventually did come across were large and asymmetrical chunks of stone that emphasized the immenseness of their enclosure: stones the size and color of dirty icebergs.

Kurt figured one such massive stone offered sufficient cover as a rest stop. He moved them over to it, and none too soon. "A light!" Laura warned, and Kurt switched off theirs.

Kurt unloaded Jim and found Laura in the darkness. Together, the two watched the wobbly light get closer.

"Left us a trail, I see; thank you very much," Marc called, apparently paused on the verge of entering the cavern; his light approached closer. "You do know, we've the manpower and firepower, not to mention the reserve supplies, to outlast you? Why not just eject your deadweight and let us all get back to normal?"

"You can have me, but let them go!" someone yelled so close to Laura that she was startled by its unexpectedness and its loudness; Kurt, who'd been wondering if he could hit anything if he fired at Marc's light still brazenly lit in the distance, was surprised, too.

"Jim!" Laura identified; she'd not heard anything from him, before this outburst, to indicate he'd regained consciousness.

"Do you hear me, Klexter?" Jim demanded. "You can have me, but *just* me!"

"Jim, please . . . " Kurt began but didn't finish; he was interrupted by a barage of incoming bullets.

Automatically, Laura ducked and asked worriedly over the noise, "Kurt?"

"Still among the living," he assured.

"Jim?" Laura demanded of their unseen companion.

The ensuing boom was earsplitting. For an instant, Laura thought they had called in cannon.

Like hail, pieces of rock rained from the unseen ceiling.

"Laura!" Kurt demanded.

Painfully pelted by falling stone, Laura crawled quickly toward his voice and collided with him. They pulled each other together and melded against the solid stone of the iceberg-like chunk they hoped would protect them from its smaller cousins.

Rocks, once they hit the ground, emitted soft "plopping" sounds as they erupted fine dust from deep, dry puddles. Laura smelled the resulting fine powder as it caught in the air and stayed there. She tasted something akin to talcum powder; the increased dust made blinking her eyes irritating and painful.

"I said you could have me?" Jim screamed, sounding delirious, from somewhere nearby.

"Jim, please!" Laura begged him to be silent and to get down. She would have gone after him, but Kurt kept her put for her own protection against still-raining stones.

The sudden "whooshing" was of hurricane proportions. Its concluding "big bang!" sent the earth into convulsive shudders and radiated dust-accompanied shock waves. The air took on a pea-soup consistency that made breathing more difficult.

"What?" Laura asked and surrendered more completely to Kurt's comforting embrace that tried so desperately to squeeze the both of them into significantly less space. "The sky is falling!"

Something hard and large bruised her already sore shoulder. Something larger ricocheted nearby and splattered buckshot-like pellets that clattered against other stones like marbles on a tin roof.

Kurt and Laura's world was ending, and Laura knew that with frightening certainty. She clung furiously to Kurt, her only consolation being that she was with him, loving him, at the end.

There was a rising cacophony: crackles, pops, bangs, whistles, pings, thuds . . .

The earth groaned in monumental bellyache, and a gigantic reverberation, then another and another, rocked the entire area.

Laura and Kurt were enveloped in the newly exploded dust.

"Kurt!" Laura moaned against his shoulder and clutched him with renewed vigor; to no avail, because the earth came farther apart at its seams, and Laura was jerked, this way and that, into suffocating, heartrending oblivion as Kurt whispered, "I love you, Laura," in her ear.

8

No doubt about it! There was the stereotypical brilliant light that signified "passing over to the other side." No mere flashlight beam could produce such a dazzling display on Laura's closed lids, not even a flashlight beam from a xenon bulb. Were Laura to open her eyes, she would surely have been blinded by it, if she weren't already beyond seeing in such an archaic manner.

There was an accompanying, cradling warmth, too. Oh, how it soothed her weary soul!

She surrendered to the light and the heat, satisfied that her time on earth hadn't seen too many sins stacked against her.

She looked forward to seeing her father and other loved ones who'd gone before her.

She regretted how her mother, left behind, would suffer, especially as Marc undoubtedly had confiscated the note left to tell the outside world where father, then daughter, had disappeared to.

Most of all, though, she regretted Kurt lost to her; strange how that heart-tugging trauma was still so painfully real when death should have put her beyond such earthbound emotions.

"Laura?": Kurt's voice.

Had he died with her, then? Would they be allowed time, after death, denied them while living?

"Thank God!" he exclaimed. "Here, let me get you out of the sun," he said. "It's moved since I left you." His hands cupped beneath her arms and dragged her a few feet to one side; then, he moved around to stand directly in front of her.

Suddenly, the light and heat dim, Laura opened her eyes and saw Kurt silhouetted against a backdrop of shimmering light bounded off swirling dust motes.

"Kurt?"

Among other things, hardly experienced by someone whisked into the Great Beyond, there were her increasing aches and pains.

"You're not dead, Laura," Kurt assured and dropped down beside her. He lowered her kerchief from around her nose and mouth and offered a drink from his canteen. Eagerly, she accepted: the water warm as it washed irritating dust all of the way down.

"I'm not dead, either," he reassured her while he watched her gulp down another swallow. He recapped the container and parenthesized her face with his free hands.

"Kiss me?" Laura said and laid her hands on his shoulders to convince herself he was flesh and blood.

"I thought you'd never ask," he said and shifted his kerchief from his face to his neck before he put his lips lingeringly against hers. He drank in her sweetness, along with the dust that covered their mouths.

"But, the light?" she asked when he lifted his mouth from hers.

"Ah, it *is* good!" he yelled, his head thrown back. In response, rock clattered somewhere; Kurt immediately put his finger to his lips. "It'd just be my luck to shout down the last of the ceiling."

"That *was* the ceiling, then, that came tumbling down?" Laura asked and shifted to alleviate more aches and pains uncovered by each passing second.

"A massive collapse," Kurt guaranteed. "It must have all been hung up there by spiderwebs, the sound of gunfire all that was needed to jar it loose. I mean, we're talking hotel-size chunks. You should see the one that apparently dropped out of that, up there." He nodded toward the hole emitting the light through the breached ceiling.

For the first time, Laura calculated just how high up that hole was. Hopes, barely realized, collapsed in an instant.

"Quite out of reach," Kurt admitted; he'd read her mind. "Even with proper rock-climbing equipment, the walls are too soft for pitons. So soft, I remain leery about sticking around here any longer than is necessary. I was scouting for an exit when I heard you call out."

"Did I call out?" Laura asked; she couldn't remember anything except . . . "What about Jim?" she asked and regretted how her smugness in survival had let her forget, even for a minute, the third member of their party.

She could tell from Kurt's expression that the news wasn't good. When he pulled Jim's watch and Daniel Kenner's I.D. bracelet out of his pocket, he verified her worst fears.

"Oh, nooooo!" she helplessly sobbed; not the least because, at the end, Jim had been so intent on trying to save Kurt and her: *You can have just me, not them!* "It just isn't fair!" She took the watch and bracelet; the watch's crystal was shattered, the mechanism dead.

"I tried for his wallet, but . . ." Kurt didn't finish.

"And what about—Marc?" she ammended.

"Good question," Kurt admitted. "There's nothing left of the tunnel entrance we came through. So, I'd guess Marc and his friends are either crushed beneath the tonnage that didn't spare that part of the cavern, or they're alive in the tunnel with no chance of getting to us."

"I hope they're not in the tunnel!" Laura said: about as close as she could come, and hoped she'd never come, to wishing anyone dead.

"It's just you and I," Kurt said.

She noticed engraving on the back of Daniel Kenner's bracelet, and she cleaned away some of the dust that filled it. Social security number? Did they have social security in Brazil? Maybe it was an anniversary or other special date? Maybe, it was a cryptic lover's code shared only by Daniel Kenner and his always-believing wife! How sad whatever the meaning it was lost forever!

"Jim was engaged to be married, did you know that?" Laura asked and more tears welled in her eyes; she figured she must look a sight and was glad she didn't have a mirror.

"No, he didn't confide in me."

"We'll give these to her, okay?" she asked and opened her hand wider to indicate the contents. "I mean, his parents are dead."

"Sure," Kurt readily agreed. He watched her carefully put the watch and the bracelet in the same pocket as her father's ring.

"With all the mysteries solved—" she said. "I'm talking the location of this cave complex, the whereabouts of our fathers, the how of our managing to make our love work. —we're left with a final mystery, aren't we?" Whatever brought Marc looking for Jim, in here of all places, when he could have had him so easily outside? Do you think Marc waited, because he knew there'd be no finding Jim's body if he left it in here? You and I know Marc wasn't really prepared to let us out to spread the tale."

"I can't begin to second-guess Marc," Kurt confessed. "Right now, the only mystery that concerns me is how to get you and me out of here alive."

"No exits, right?" she ventured; it wouldn't surprise her. She refused to be too "up," because she felt toyed with by forces beyond her control; as the high opening, teasing with its streaming sunlight, was evidence to support her case.

"Actually, I did find a way out," Kurt surprised. "Out of *here,* this cavern, at least," he ammended. "I'm hoping it's a new route opened to the outside when the roof fell."

"Yes, that would be best," Laura agreed. Why was a new route preferable to one already there before? For the reason neither Kurt nor Laura put into words: it seemed inconceivable that Karl Reiger, not killed by the tunnel cave-in, wouldn't have explored every possible exit before he came back to the one he knew, for a fact, accessed the outside world—if he could only dig his way through the blockage. Unless . . .

"My father may have been injured by the tunnel cave-in," Kurt said; once again, he'd read her mind; his knack for doing that was only enhanced by the love that now bound them together. "Maybe, a broken leg. Maybe, a debilitating head injury. It'll take an expert to tell, after twenty-four years, and I'm no forensics expert."

"Yes, maybe he was injured," Laura agreed, because she wanted so desperately to believe. Surely, Kurt and she hadn't gotten this far, endured so much, to be deprived of their happy-ever-after ending.

"You think you're up to some hiking?" Kurt asked, made nervous by the sounds of more cascading stones.

"The sooner we're out, the sooner we can tell the

authorities," Laura said and let Kurt help her, so stiff it hurt, to her feet. All around, there was the seemingly perpetual dust-fall that Laura found increasingly oppressive. Kurt and she were like cookies overly dusted with powdered sugar after baking. Was this how they'd look, if given half the chance to reach old age: gray hair, gray skin? She was sure Kurt looked better than she did. Nor would gallons of soap and water wash from her all the residue of this thoroughly frightening experience.

If their stuff bag had disappeared in the rubble, Kurt had been lucky enough to salvage their light, and a good thing too; the sunlight, pouring through the ruptured ceiling, didn't penetrate the tunnel they soon stooped to enter. A mere few feet into this latest hole, Laura wished to return to the sunlight, even if that sunlight tortured with hints of a world still beyond their reach.

"Maybe, someone heard the collapse," Laura said and stopped. "Maybe, they're there, now, looking down through the hole."

"There's an awful lot of jungle up there, Laura," Kurt logically argued. "You've seen it: acres and acres of impassable undergrowth. And, here's but one hole suddenly appeared somewhere in the middle of it. Granted, it's a sizable hole, but how big in comparison to the expanse of wilderness extending outward around it in all directions? However, just in case, I left my T-shirt draped over the rock immediately below the hole. I put a note in the pocket that detailed where we've gone."

"Good thinking," Laura admitted. She should have known he'd covered all the bases.

She took the hand he offered her, following him deeper into the tunnel.

The low ceiling of the tunnel made their progress less easy than it might have been. Aside from the constant stooping it required, though, the passageway proved uneventful. It held no unsavory surprises and was monotonous in its absence of branchings, caverns, galleries, or even tumor-like appendages.

"You know," Kurt said at their first rest break, "it's conceivable my father never did thoroughly explore all the possibilities, for other reasons than that he was injured by the cave-in. All, or most of his provisions might have been buried. All of his effort might have been devoted to digging out his friends. No food, maybe no water, plus frustrated exhaustion, might have done him in."

"I'll be delighted to entertain that thought," Laura granted. "I'd love to think this didn't lead your father to the same dead-end it might yet lead us to."

She took a swallow from her canteen, thankful she had water. A person could survive for weeks without food, but try it without anything to drink. She only wished they'd run across a fresh supply.

Two days later, after the tunnel *finally* expanded its height so they could walk upright, and expanded its width so they could walk side by side without rubbing shoulders, Laura got her wish. At first, she was prepared to believe the roaring was another flood; no way would she survive the wild ride back to the sun-breached cavern.

"Cascades up ahead!" Kurt assured. He knew she thought flood, because he'd thought the same thing. However, he'd heard enough underground streams, during the course of his spelunking career, to put correct definition to this one, as had Laura, at least in retrospect.

"I thought for sure we walked a dry hole," Laura said with a thank-Heaven-I-was-mistaken tone of voice. "We haven't seen water since we swam in: deluge or drought, since feast or famine doesn't fit the bill quite as well."

"A full belly of water will help staunch our hunger pains," Kurt predicted; Laura and he had eased off on their water ration, over the last couple of days, in case they weren't lucky.

They approached with caution, as well they might; more than one unwitting spelunker had misjudged in the dark and stepped into the drink, sometimes with dire consequences.

The cascades were of a size and force that made conversation impossible anywhere in their immediate vicinity. The deluge rushed across the tunnel at a right angle and, over the years, had washed out sizable amounts of limestone at its entrance and exit points. Its entrance was the less mutilated, because an intrusion of igneous rock had resisted erosion to form steep steps, down over which the water flushed in a furious and rapid boil. The water, then, sluiced under a narrow, natural bridge and, still boiling, was expelled on the other side. The torrent continued pell-mell along a gouged trough-like groove that was a good fifteen-feet across, and seemingly bottomless. The force of the water collided with a seemingly dead-end wall; but, the minimum of splash and no back up or flooding said the wall had at least one submerged hole to feed all that water somewhere.

The narrow bridge looked solid, but looks could deceive. Kurt, the heavier of the duo, motioned he'd go first.

There was never any question that forward was their only alternative, since nothing existed for them behind. Unfortunately, there was no other way forward but over the water; that meant the bridge, because jumping or swimming the boil was out of the question. Even so, Laura was haunted by the prospect of the bridge collapsing and Kurt a victim. Even if Kurt and she had a rope to link one to the other, the force of the water, upon anyone committed to its violence, would have pulled the other in.

For Laura, though, dying with Kurt had become preferable to living without him in this hopelessly endless hole in the ground. So, she insisted he hold her hand as he worked his way slowly out over the water. He, in turn, insisted she let go once she was on the verge of becoming dangerously overextended.

No longer his anchor, as flimsy as that anchor might have been, Laura bit her fingernails: a bad habit once cured, with some difficulty, years before.

Kurt continued to put one foot slowly in front of the other, cautiously adding his full weight to his lead foot and, finally, pausing for any telltale signs or vibrations he might interpret as a warning. He kept his light flashed, in quick succession, on where his feet were, where they would be next, and where they'd have to jump if worse turned to worst.

If the roaring had been less deafening, Laura would have heard Kurt's whoop of joy upon his reaching the other side. As it was, she had to be content with her own exhalation of air held so long inside of her that she'd been on the verge of turning blue.

Her stomach fluttered with butterflies now that she was expected to follow. As she focused on the bridge, its width seemed to narrow visibly in direct proportion to the seeming expansion of its length: something right out of *Alice in Wonderland:* an illusion of the light Kurt had aimed back onto her side of the torrent.

The same beam spotlighted her feet as she began, ever so slowly, to feel her way across the expanse of wet stone.

"Piece of cake!" she mumbled uncertainly. She'd successfully crossed a good many such natural bridges in her time; some over water, some over hard rock, some over seemingly nothing at all. She had a good sense of timing and balance, proved time and time again. She had honed her confidence, over the years, to what she'd always imagined, in such circumstances, was the same enjoyed by high-steel walkers who strolled the girders of unfinished skyscrapers. So, why was her heart in her throat?

"Because," she distinctly thought when she realized the

bridge was coming apart beneath her; "somehow Kurt and I just aren't meant to be!"

She might have managed a successful jump backward, although probably not; anyway, it wasn't any longer simple self-preservation that motivated her.

So, she made a valiant attempt to reach Kurt, and she actually touched his hand which was desperately outstretched for her. However, their touch was painfully fleeting, however, as the rock bridge, possibly stress-fractured when subjected to Kurt's weight, dropped like the trapdoor of a gallows beneath her.

Laura took a deep breath as if she were undergoing finals for a high-school swimming class. Unfortunately, the immediate beating she took from the water that pitilessly swallowed her was enough to knock all of her reserve air right out of her.

Apparently, it was becoming another of her recurring nightmares, like the lock combination unremembered, or the test unstudied, or the housework undone . . .

Only this was worse!

She was trapped, once again, in a maelstrom of water; there was no air, but there were hard, sharp objects that banged, cut, battered.

It was all the same roaring, choking, gasping, pummeling, grappling: all the same drowning.

It was as if she were downed in a full sink without its plug. On the way down the drain, she got caught, but the water violently stuffed her on through, and it kept on stuffing until she was launched on a slideway more complex and meandering than any at Bunyan Water Slides Park outside Phoenix. That teeth-rattling corkscrew ride aborted in a dizzying drop into space filled with welcome air as well as water.

When her feet hit, they rammed into something that yielded

only after her legs buckled and her knees savagely hit her chin.

Partially unconscious, she still had some instinctive need to live, because an inner voice demanded, "Kick, Laura, kick!"

Did she have the energy, though, to kick? Yes, but for how long? Frankly, she was surprised when it was long enough to propel her head clear of the water. "Aggggggh!" she gasped appreciatively for long-denied breath.

It took long, additional minutes, and more kicks, before she realized she'd surfaced in an eddy of a large underground pool.

If she mustered the effort to attempt reaching the nearest rim of the pool, it was only because it would have been ironic to come this distance only to fail with a rest stop so near at hand. She asked of herself nothing more than to progress one small inch at a time. If she, more than once, thought another inch impossible to achieve, memories of Kurt, waiting for her somewhere, egged her on.

A seeming eternity later, her fingertips unbelievably touched solid rock, and she clung desparately to the shoreline. She knew if she let go, she'd sink below the depths once and for all.

Even when she got her second wind, it took her four attempts to leave the water that still seemed anxious to have her; it held her back like viscous glue.

Once landed, like a beached and dying whale, she crawled over hard rock that further bruised her bruised knees, and she hoisted herself up and over a small, pillow-shaped rock, her head and arms draped over the opposite side.

"Oh, Kurt, where are you, and where am I?" she groaned, and her jaw hurt as her words formed bubbles at her pouted lips.

She shut her eyes, and collapsed. When she opened them, she felt better, if not entirely alive.

Ever so slowly, she righted herself into a sitting position. For the first time, she became aware of an overall view of the pool and the water that, pouring from a chimney-like hole in the ceiling, filled the pool. She knew, just by looking, that she'd been ejected through that hole; she remembered the jarring at touchdown. She was only surprised she hadn't, then, been swept away in the channel that emptied the excess water a few yards away.

The waterfall, pool, runoff, and a surrounding forest of stone, were part of a natural cavern. Seeing all of it so clearly, Laura was struck by the miracle of seeing it at all, since nothing was concealed by customary total darkness.

There were caves — in New Zealand, she thought — illuminated by larvae that produced cold light, not unlike that of a firefly. Was that the case here?

She stood and took hold of a nearby chunk of hard, black stone for balance. Her dizziness, considering what she'd been through, was surely par for the course. Nevertheless, the hand she put to her forehead felt a decided bump where there shouldn't have been one. A concussion? She didn't think so, because she remembered her name, she remembered Jim dead. She remembered Kurt . . . Oh, Kurt!

Wobbly, she headed for the nearest wall. Once she reached it, she saw that it was made of hard basalt, not of soft limestone. A closer check of her surroundings revealed to her that all of the rock formations were of igneous rock, none of the softer limestone with which she'd become so familiar over the last few days.

Laura's breath caught in her throat as, out of the corner of her eye, she spotted a distant semicircle of brightness. Every rock formation between it and her was back-lit by it. She was drawn to it like iron filings drawn to a magnet. It invited with promises of sunshine and exit: a way to Captain Fortuna-Mata, a way to a search party that could be dropped through the hole in the forest floor, a way back to Kurt, a way back to a love.

As, off to her right, the sound of running water hinted how the runoff from the pool was apparently paralleling Laura's route, the distance beckoned with an additional enticement that made Laura salivate as helplessly as any Pavlov dog. She moaned, "Oh, please, yes!" and leaned, weak-kneed, against the wall. "Roasting meat!" she disbelievingly identified.

She pushed off, instilled with a new burst of energy and willpower, because roasting meat meant people, maybe a radio, Captain Fortuna-Mata, a search party, Kurt . . .

In her anxiousness, she almost died at the end. Fatigue-slowed reflexes barely stopped her on the brink of the same ledge over which the channeled water from the pool, emerging from a jumble of rocks a few yards to Laura's right, plunged to the lower level.

Below her, the water that had exited the cavern pool finally escaped through a large light-filled opening that gave way to readily accessible jungle. Laura thought she'd never been so happy to see jungle.

She was happier yet to see the camp fire, meat roasting, and
. . .

Two men sat on the rocks almost directly below her. Two more men squatted on their haunches at the lip of the cave and looked out over the verdant landscape.

Off to one side, in the shadows, two other men . . .

"Oh!" Laura gasped as she defined Jean-Michael and Joe tied to a limestone column. She stepped back, stumbled, and kicked loose stones over the edge. She heard the resulting clatter of rock against rock. More ominous, she heard the muffled comments of one or more of the men below. Distinctive sounds told her that someone was coming to investigate.

Laura hurriedly retreated. She had to find someplace to hide, somewhere by herself where she could decide what it meant finding Jean-Michael and Joe held captive down below.

Joe should have been back at the runway by now. And, what of Jean-Michael? Had he really been mauled by a jaguar, or . . . ?

". . . wild-goose chase!" someone said and interrupted Laura's reverie.

Laura backed into a shadowy recess and held her breath. The shadows weren't nearly deep enough to make her really secure; what she wouldn't have given for a bit of the total darkness she'd so recently left behind.

"How many times have we checked this out?" the same voice asked; Laura couldn't see him. "There's no way in from back here, remember?"

"So, no one said you had to come with me, right?" someone else challenged.

"We're all getting paranoid; let's face it. I, for one, will be glad when Marc and Kempner get back with the merchandise."

References to Marc didn't make Laura feel any safer. She backed deeper into the shadows but stopped when she saw the two young, handsome blond men walk slowly past.

Then, she heard the faint sound behind her and would have automatically turned to confront whatever or whomever made it, except a clammy hand tightly slapped itself over her mouth, a clamp-like arm wrapped her waist, and she was tightly pulled back against something wet, hard, and graveyard cold.

"Shhhhhh!" the warning was hissed in Laura's ear and relayed more than a mere expulsion of breath. That she couldn't really believe it was Kurt didn't mean she was willing to betray even that possibility by squealing for help from the already known enemy.

"I suppose you didn't hear that, Karl?" one of the enemy asked sarcastically; he and his companion had moved out of sight.

"Hear what, Jurgen? Steam? Or, more likely, a snake that might hiss as well as move pebbles?"

"I hate snakes!"

"They're no more fond of us, my friend. So, if you're intent upon running this one to ground, count me out. I'd rather finish my meal." He momentarily came into view, headed back the way he'd come.

Jurgen followed but stopped right abreast of the shadow-filled recess that contained Laura. He turned directly to face her; Laura would have groaned despair, except the protective arm around her middle warned her into continued silence with the tightening of its already breath-depriving squeeze.

"Jurgen?" Karl called. "You coming, or what?"

"Wait up?" Jurgen instructed and was gone.

Laura silently thanked the darkness for being mercifully sufficient. At the same time, she listened to be sure the enemy's retreat was a real one.

Finally, the hand on her mouth fell away.

She turned and asked, "Kurt?"

She knew what she saw: his face muted by shadow; his eyes, his mouth, his chin. "Oh, Kurt," she moaned and disbelievingly added: "Is it you?"

His answer was to take her in his arms and kiss her. His heart still beat wildly from their close call.

Laura still couldn't believe the miracle. How could it be possible?

"This way," Kurt whispered and took her hand. He led her through a maze of shadowy, rock formations.

The sound of water got louder, until Kurt and Laura reached the channel of pool runoff and turned right toward the greater roar of water dropped through the chimney.

"We can talk here," Kurt said when he felt the water noises sufficient to mask their own.

Laura was too happy for talk. Rather, she slid her arms around his waist and held on, still not positive he was real.

"Life without you holds no meaning," Kurt said and ran his hands up and down her arms. "So, I followed you — wherever."

"You could have been killed," she said and got chills at the thought.

He didn't deny it: "Almost was," he admitted. "Got plugged into this small hole, like a cork plugged in the neck of a bottle. Water pressure and shedding my gun made the difference, but I'll probably have scratches and stretch marks as forever-after reminders. However, it was *all* worth it!"

He took her hand and pulled her down beside him on a rock. Their only light remained the diffused flow that reached them along the straight runway of water; still, it was bright compared to the dark they were used to.

"I came barreling down out of the ceiling, straight into the pool and immediately got dumped over the spillway," he detailed. "I was washed by the runoff to — " He pointed out where the matter made its final distant tumble before flowing outside. " — there. Luckily, 'there' is boulder-strewn, or I would have belly flopped on the rocks below. Wouldn't that have surprised a few people?"

"You know they have Jean-Michael and Joe?"

"I'd just spotted those two through a crack in some rocks when I was distracted by you, spied through another crack, as you made your precarious balancing act on the lip of the ledge. Talk about a heart-stopper!"

"Imagine what my heart was doing at the time," Laura challenged.

"I thought I could head you off, but those two got too close before I dared scream, 'Here I am!' Then, when you obviously sensed me so close, not likely to know who I was, I figured it had to be a more unconventional hello. Sorry if I scared you."

"I should be so scared every day," she said, took both of his hands in hers and gave a squeeze.

"When that bridge collapsed, I thought we'd seen the last of each other," he said and kissed one of her hands, then the other.

"Ye of little faith!"

"As soon as it's dark, I figure to give Jean-Michael and Joe a surprise visit," Kurt said and delivered another loving kiss to her fingers. "Kind of a one-man storming of the Bastille."

"Meaning," Laura divined, her intuition working overtime, "you expect me to wait here."

"One of us has to pull me out of the fire if I muff up the rescue," Kurt reasoned. "Besides, we've only one gun between us, mine lost on the ride in."

"And you think my gun still works?"

"Whether it does or not, it'll look more impressive than if I point my finger and go, 'Bang! Bang!'"

"I suppose you're not prepared to take no for an answer?"

"No."

"There's something I should remember about double negatives, but, lucky for one of us, it escapes me at the moment. If I'm frankly too bushed to play cops and robbers, though, I wish you were, too."

"We'll have better odds with Jean-Michael and Joe put in action."

"Did you hear Karl and Jurgen mention that Marc and someone called Kempner are on the way?"

"Anyway, so they *think*," Kurt qualified. "However, even if that is the case, remember that we took a shortcut. Marc and Kempner have jungle with which to contend."

"I wish them bad luck," Laura said. She unbuckled her holster and handed it, and her gun, over. "You, I wish good luck."

"Well, I can't complain so far," he said and pulled her onto his cushioning lap. "Things could be much worse."

"Yes, there is that," she admitted and wrapped her arms

around his neck. "Just tell me how things are going to be even better."

"They're going to be even better," he guaranteed and kissed her.

Reassured by Kurt's presence and by their ensuing blissful hours of warmth-inducing hugging, Laura felt sorry she hadn't argued more forcefully to accompany him. As it was, he refused to let her go back on their original plan. It apparently made no difference to him that, were he discovered, the enemy would surely make a thorough search of the premises, and Laura would be hard-pressed to find a place to hide; there was no way back up that chimney, a la Santa Claus.

"You stay put, even if you hear gunshots," he told her; she got a bad chill at the sounds of that. "Without your gun, you'll just be another vulnerable target. If you have to come on a rescue mission, make sure you give them time to think I came at them alone. Okay?"

Laura was noncommittal; as far as she was concerned, he'd gotten one too many promises from her already.

She watched him disappear into the shadows and rocks, and she was more convinced that, whatever they were doing, they should be doing it together. Too often they'd been separated, lucky to get back together; their luck was possibly running out.

Gunfire, when it came, convinced her, all the more, that they'd made the wrong decision. She was little reassured by accompanying shouts of surprise. How did she know it wasn't Kurt who made them?

She nestled deeper into her niche and resisted all impulse to leave it. Kurt was right: she didn't have a gun and would be no help whatsoever unless she was able, if and when required, to sneak up later.

However, when she heard the gunshots stop, their having lasted far beyond any limit that Laura found acceptable, she was even more convinced and resentful. If Kurt had died, it was Laura's place to have been with him. He hadn't hidden himself in a hole when the bridge had collapsed and dumped her in the water.

She crawled out of her concealment and wished she hadn't been persuaded to crawl into it, in the first place.

"Laura?" she was greeted.

She wrapped his waist and squeezed with a vigor that made her bruised and battered body ache in protest.

He rained a deluge of sweet kisses over her face. "They weren't expecting an assault from inside the cave. As a result, I had a far easier time, than I ever thought possible, in getting Jean-Michael and Joe untied. After that, we rushed the couple inside the cave for their guns. Final head count: the three of us fine; two of them dead; the other two, not liking the whittled-down odds, hightailed it into the jungle. Jean-Michael is on their abandoned radio, now, trying to reach Captain Fortuna-Mata to head the bad guys off at the pass. Joe is on guard at the mouth of the cave in case they decide to return, with or without Marc and Kempner in reenforcement. By the way, welcome to deNali!"

"Tell me I'm not dreaming!" Laura begged and her hugging arms refused to let him go.

"Would a decent meal convince you?" Kurt tempted playfully. "They left behind a good many leftovers, not the least of which was some of the meat."

"Who let you in on the secret that the way to a woman's heart is through her stomach?" Laura asked and her stomach, on cue, gave an embarrassingly growl.

"Mmmmmm, even *that* sounds beautiful to my ears; it must be love!"

"It *is* love!" Laura assured and took his hand. "Until we can do something more about it, let's eat!"

"Right this way, ma'am," he directed, but Laura led the way.

"Laura!" Jean-Michael greeted when he spotted her on the ledge; he gave a wave. Apparently in good spirits, and good shape, he certainly didn't look as if he'd been mauled and half-eaten by a jungle cat, and he probably hadn't; Marc, among his other talents, was obviously a consummate liar. More likely, Jean-Michael and Joe had been kidnap victims.

Joe waved from the mouth of the cave, and Jean-Michael announced, "The captain is on his way!"

"Marvelous news!" Kurt complimented.

"Please, then, let me get to the food," Laura begged. "I've seen the captain eat, remember?"

"Right!" Kurt concurred but took time for another long kiss before he led her down one of several steep pathways to the lower level.

9

She answered his knock, delivered a hello kiss, and begged, "Please give me a few more minutes. I'm afraid I'm still not used to water not out to drown me; lounging in the tub made me lose all sense of time."

"You look irresistibly marvelous!" he told her.

"Compliments will get you *almost* anything," she promised; it was wonderful to be out of the jungle, in a hotel with modern conveniences, with the blush on her skin from a hot bath and the tingle on her lips from Kurt's kiss, "but me looking like this will get us both kicked out of the hotel dining room."

Actually, as verified by the bathroom mirror, she didn't look all that bad—everything considered. Her new clothes hid most of her nasty bruises and welts. Foundation and makeup, a few shades darker than what she'd normally use, concealed most of the ravages to her face; her one night back in civilization had proved an even more effective eraser of fatigue lines. The hotel beautician had even managed a respectable job on Laura's hair. All Laura really needed was a wet line of perfume along her neck, another along each of her forearms, and . . .

"Any word about 'our friends the botanists'?" she called.

"Jurgen Miesen and Karl Pughner, both students, are the two dead," Kurt answered. "Not a trace of Kempner Klyne, or of Marc. No sign, either, of Professor Denlick and the other student, Petre Rudolph; both escaped during the shooting. They were all bonafide members of a Universidad de Asuncion plant-finding team, all right; although no one at the university knows anything about a moss that supposedly has potential for immune system research. Captain Fortuna-Mata suspects it was all an elaborate cover, probably to do with the illegal smuggling of archaelogical artifacts out of the country. Unfortunately, it's doubtful any of the missing group will turn up back at the university to answer our questions; the captain figures there was likely a preplanned escape route in case of just the kind of interference you and I provided. As for their insisting that they only wanted Jim, that was undoubtedly a ploy to sucker us in for easier killing."

There was a knock at the door, and Kurt went to answer it. Laura replaced the stopper in her perfume flacon and joined Kurt and their visitor.

The visitor in question had long red hair, cool blue eyes, a model's cheekbones, and a small mole on her chin that many would call a beauty mark. She was dressed in fashionable white linen.

Immediately, Laura wanted to go back into the bathroom for another once-over.

"Laura Lexly, Sarah Maxwell," Kurt introduced.

"Jim's financée?" Laura put title to the name.

"I hope you don't mind my stopping by unannounced," Sarah said. "I was here in Manaus, waiting for Jim, when the bad news came over the television. I understand both of you were with him at the last."

"Do you know why Marc Klexter wanted Jim dead?" Laura asked.

Sarah's pretty face wasn't nearly so pretty when screwed up in a grimace. "I thought he was killed in a cave-in."

"Haven't you talked to Brazilian authorities?" Laura asked, her surprise evident. "I suspect they'll be quite anxious to talk with you, since you're here."

"I'm afraid, since the bad news, I've been indisposed."

"You really should contact Captain Fortuna-Mata, first thing," Laura counseled; Kurt, usually on Laura's wavelength, was getting strange vibes.

"Of course," Sarah accepted. "Until then, I just thought Jim might have said something at the last, or . . ." She shrugged, unzipped her fashion-coordinated white purse and pulled out a white hanky. She dabbed at her eyes.

"Actually, we brought back his watch and his father's I.D. bracelet, thinking you might like to have them," Kurt said and wondered why Laura seemed less than sympathetic.

"Yes," Laura quickly admitted. "The Brazilian authorities promised to turn Jim's personal things over to us, since he has no immediate family. We've always planned to pass them on to you." Kurt watched Laura carefully and gave a questioning uplift of his left eyebrow. "Where can we reach you?" Laura asked.

"I'm staying at the Amazonas."

"As soon as we get Jim's things, then, we'll let you know," Laura assured.

"You say, his watch and his father's I.D. bracelet?"

"There'll undoubtedly be more once they return with his body," Kurt elucidated. "At the time of his death . . . Well, the circumstances were such that . . ." He left it at that.

"I do appreciate your consideration," Sarah said. "Now, it

does look as if I've interrupted something, and I do apologize; I really should have called."

"We'd be pleased to have you join us for supper," Kurt invited.

"By all means," Laura seconded but sounded as less-than-enthusiastic as she was.

"I think it'll be another supper alone in my hotel room, although I appreciate the offer," Sarah opted. "I'm really not up to facing the general public quite yet." She walked to the door, Kurt and Laura in attendance. "Jim did warn me that going into the Brazilian jungle wasn't the same as going to the local botanical gardens for a Sunday picnic. However, as much as I thought he was prepared . . ." She finished off with more dabs of her eyes with her hanky.

"We'll call you," Laura repeated and opened the door.

"Thank you," Sarah said and stepped into the hallway.

Laura closed the door between them.

"Want to tell me what that was about, Miss Hard-Heart?" Kurt asked. It had taken all of his willpower not to ask while Sarah was in the room.

Laura put a finger to her lips for silence and leaned an ear against the door. After a minute, in which a surprised Kurt looked on, Laura opened the door and looked out. Only when she turned back did she answer: "That woman was no more Jim's fiancée than I was."

"You're sure?" he asked and wondered how she could be.

"Jim showed me a photograph. Miss Stepped-from-the-Pages-of-a-Fashion-Magazine, red hair or no, wasn't the woman in it," Laura assured him.

"Which is why you said the authorities have Jim's watch and his father's I.D. bracelet when you still have them?"

"What I said was, 'The Brazilian authorities promised us Jim's personal things.' Which they have."

"I think the lady misunderstood that to mean they presently have *all* Jim's possessions, or will have as soon as they recover his body."

"She can think what she pleases," Laura said and went to the phone. "In the meantime . . ." She picked up the phone and asked for an overseas operator.

"Overseas means you're not calling Captain Fortuna-Mata," Kurt surmised.

"Not quite yet," Laura admitted. "I'm hoping for a bit more to give him."

She remembered how Jim had said the kibbutz where he'd met Sarah was near Metulla.

"Metulla, Israel?" Kurt echoed, his curiosity rampant.

"The real Sarah Maxwell is Jewish," Laura admitted.

"And Jim?"

Laura shrugged. "He never told me; I never asked. He probably would have never mentioned Sarah if I hadn't caught him off guard."

"Which explains why he never bothered mentioning her to me?"

"He didn't think it was pertinent. Was it?"

"Guess not," he decided. "Not now, anyway."

"Right?" Laura agreed and went back to trying to find Sarah Maxwell at one of the several kibbutzes that turned out to be near Metulla. A woman at the third one contacted knew Sarah's present whereabouts.

"Something?" Kurt asked from the chair he'd taken at ringside.

"Sarah is on an archaelogical dig in the Israeli Negev," Laura said. "I've got her father's number, though."

A few minutes later, she got through to Seth Maxwell: "Mr. Maxwell?" she asked the man who answered. "My name is Laura Lexly. I'm trying to reach your daughter, Sarah. It's bad news, I'm afraid, about her fiancé, Jim Kenner."

"He's dead, isn't he?" Seth Maxwell said.

"I'm afraid he is, yes," Laura admitted and wondered what he knew that she didn't.

"I told them they'd kill him," Seth said and sounded genuinely regretful.

"Told whom, Mr. Maxwell?" Laura pressed, determined to make her call worth it.

"Where are you calling from, Miss Lexly?" he asked; he'd ignored her query.

"Manaus, Brazil, Mr. Maxwell." Then to pique his curiosity, she added: "I was just visited by a young woman who said she was your daughter, but she looked nothing like the photograph of Sarah that Jim showed me."

"Give me your number, Miss Lexly, and I'll get back to you in a few hours' time."

"I'm staying at the Tropical Hotel Manaus. Room three-oh-four."

The phone went dead; just like that.

"Well?" Kurt asked.

"He's promised to get back to me in a few hours."

"Would you prefer we order room service, so we don't miss his return call?"

"Would you mind?"

"Aside from being just as curious as you, it doesn't matter to me where I eat, or what I eat, just as long as I'm with you," he said with a grin. "What do you suppose our pseudo Miss Maxwell is up to?"

"And, why do you suppose the real Sarah's father wasn't surprised Jim was dead?"

"*Mixira.*"

"*Mixira?*"

"A local dish of manatee meat," Kurt said. "Since I have no

other answers, it's what I propose to have for supper."

"Make that for two," Laura said and handed him the phone.

Later, they were at the table rolled in for them and left by room service, each savoring the indescribable flavors of *mixira*, when the four gunmen came through the door.

It wasn't like television: no shotgun blasts, no wood and glass splintered. Somehow, they'd simply and silently picked the lock, or maybe had a key.

Each wore black rubber-soled shoes, black pants, a black turtleneck sweater, and a black stocking mask with crudely cut mouth and eye holes. Each carried a gun; two of the guns were designed for rapid automatic fire.

The four were no sooner in the room, one demanding in a no-nonsense manner that Kurt and Laura "Get facedown on the floor!", another heading into the bedroom, another heading into the bathroom, than the fourth pulled the door shut behind them; it couldn't have taken longer than a very few seconds.

"What's this all . . . ?" Kurt, on the floor beside Laura, started to ask but wasn't given the chance to finish.

"Keep your mouth shut, or I'l have to shut it for you!" he was warned.

Laura's world telescoped to include Kurt and a bottom-up view of black-clad legs, and she smelled the stench of a once-used chemical carpet cleaner. She wondered why, snatched finally from a hostile cave and jungle, they had to have danger follow them here. She was sure it had something to do with the missing Marc and with the pseudo Sarah Maxwell.

As she watched, she saw three of the four gunmen leave as quickly and as silently as they'd entered.

"Sorry about this," the one remaining said, holstered her gun, and doffed her face mask; Laura heard the apology over the frantic beat of her heart. "It was necessary," their uninvited visitor concluded, "that we discern if this was some kind of setup."

"Setup?" Kurt challenged loudly, and he was boiling mad. He wasn't pleased that it all happened so fast that he'd been powerless.

"Kurt?" Laura tried, but Kurt was on a roll.

"You'd better have a good explanation," he warned and dared scramble to his feet; somehow, non-chauvinist that he was, he was furious to find this partial cause of his heart stuck in his throat was a woman, "or you're going to find yourself in trouble with more than the Brazilian authorities?"

"Kurt?" Laura tried again.

"Kurt Reiger; Sarah Maxwell," Laura introduced and gave him the kind of hug she hoped relayed her awareness that there was nothing either of them could have done. "The *real* Sarah Maxwell," she added, as if Kurt might somehow confuse the two.

"I thought the *real* Sarah Maxwell was on an archaelogical dig in Israel," Kurt reminded.

"A necessary ruse to allow me to wait for Jim here in Manaus," Sarah explained, "and keep certain people from the truth. As it's difficult for nosy people to go unobserved for long in the Negev, people who came looking for me there would stand out like sore thumbs for the friends I have waiting to intercept them."

"Who exactly did you expect to come looking for you there, Miss Maxwell?" Kurt wanted to know.

"The same people who killed Jim for his father's I.D. bracelet," Sarah admitted. "Had they *not* gotten the bracelet, it's likely they might have forcefully tried to pick me up as part of an exchange for it."

"What's so important about Daniel Kenner's I.D. bracelet?" Kurt demanded. He wasn't pacified or satisfied by a long shot.

"It's what they were after and what, I presume, they got,"

Sarah explained.

She motioned them onto the couch, and she took the chair opposite them.

"Once again, my apologies for the sweep we just made of your hotel room," she said. "While my father seemed convinced your call about a visit from a 'pseudo-me' was genuine, we had to be sure. The people who killed Jim would be just as pleased to see me and my friends dead. I'm only sorry we didn't trust you with an explanation earlier." She shrugged. "Unfortunately, that's only realized in retrospect."

"The way I see it, we don't have much of an explanation, even now," Kurt challenged.

Sarah ran her fingers through long, orange hair that was disarrayed from its recent stuffing into the stocking mask. "I don't know how much you know about Jim and his parents' background . . ."

"Why don't you presume we know nothing," Kurt interrupted.

"Jim assumed that was the case, as it had been for your fathers before you. However, there was all that business in the press about Karl Reiger's possible Nazi connections—which gave us pause."

Kurt was suddenly as leery of the real Sarah Maxwell as Laura had been of the fake one.

"Jim's grandparents immigrated from Germany to Brazil, prior to the outbreak of World War II," Sarah obliged, 'but they retained connections with friends and acquaintances in the Fatherland who later rose to prominence in the Nazi movement. After the war, Jim's father was in the right place, at the right time, to be recruited by an organization whose sole purpose was to get surviving high-ranking party members safely out of postwar Europe. Daniel was given access to large sums of currency, gems, and precious metals, some of which were brought out by escaping Nazis, some of which was donated to the cause. A lot of it was 'laundered' under Daniel's supervision through various financial and international institutions in order to 'muddy the waters' for Nazi hunters out to bring war criminals to justice and stop all succor to the Nazis, financial or otherwise.

"Daniel was personally responsible for a particularly large sum, stashed in a numbered Swiss bank account, that supported several Nazi bigwigs incommunicado in South America. When Daniel turned up missing, the number of that Swiss account came up missing with him.

"There were accusations and suspicions, within the group, that Daniel had absconded with the money. His wife, on the other hand, remained convinced his disappearance was unrelated.

"The problem: Daniel, an avid spelunker, had kept the particulars of his subterranean-cave discovery a secret, even from his wife. He'd jealously not wanted anyone to exploit it before he did.

"Mrs. Kenner told Jim what she knew about his father's and her part in the organization, and she died shortly thereafter. Jim, disgusted by the role of his parents, sought personal atonement by conversion to Judaism on a kibbutz in northern Israel. That's where I met him and where we . . ." She didn't finish the thought but said, instead: "He was in Israel when word reached us of the discovery of the last campsite. He arranged for you to join him on the expedition, hoping to benefit from your input; and I, with some of my people, made arrangements to wait for him here, in case he needed help getting the bracelet, if recovered, out of the country."

"How ironic that Jim's father was the Nazi sympathizer, after all the accusations made against Karl Reiger," Laura commented and gave Kurt's arm a sympathetic squeeze.

"What, though, does Daniel Kenner's I.D. bracelet have to

do with any of this?" Kurt wanted to know, more than ever.

"The number of that nefarious Swiss bank account, at least according to Jim's mother, is engraved on the back of it," Sarah informed.

"Oh!" Laura exclaimed, her hand suddenly at her mouth.

Laura handed over the broken watch and the engraved I.D. bracelet, and tears immediately formed in Sarah's blue eyes. Sarah allowed herself a full minute of visible grief before she wiped her eyes, blew her nose, and then wrote down the numbers from the back of the bracelet into a small notebook she pulled from the buttoned front pocket of her turtleneck sweater.

"Now," she said, "one more favor, if you please." She extended the watch and the bracelet back to Laura. "Would you call the fake Sarah Maxwell, and have her come pick these up before she tries her let's-pretend act out on the Brazilian authorities and learns Kurt and you have been holding out on her?"

Laura and Kurt were confused, and their expressions showed it.

Sarah took advantage to keep the watch and bracelet a moment longer and explained: "It's this way. With the number of the Swiss bank account, we could pirate the funds, and that would certainly be a blow to the enemy's cause. Except, they've not had access to those funds for twenty-four years, and they've undoubtedly made other arrangements to work around them; not that they aren't eager to reclaim what they assume is rightfully theirs. On the other hand, if we know the number, let the enemy know the number, and, then, closely monitor all future deposits and withdrawals, noting who makes which, and where the money comes from and goes to, we stand a chance of ferreting out all kinds of useful information we couldn't hope to obtain otherwise. You can't kill a Hydra until you identify every head. Do you see? What we have is something with far more potential than a mere bank account."

"Was it worth Jim dying for?" Laura asked, because Jim had been her friend, and she missed him.

"He made the decision," Sarah reminded. "I always implicitly trusted his judgment; he knew the risks."

"You want us to call this woman now?" Kurt asked. He admired Jim's ability to die for his principles, and he was prepared to do everything he could to make that death worthwhile.

"Yes, please," Sarah instructed. "Tell her, if you would, that the Brazilian authorities brought the watch and I.D. bracelet by shortly after she left you."

Laura placed the call.

Within the hour, the woman — pseudo Sarah Maxwell — was again in Laura's hotel room: "I can't tell you how much this means to me," she said and dropped the bracelet into her purse. She kept the broken watch in her hand and went through the motions of cherishing the feel of it; apparently, someone had given her acting lessons during the last few hours. She even managed a couple of tears.

However, Laura remained completely unimpressed. In truth, she had a strong impulse to bash the phony. Instead, she said: "We'll see you get the rest of Jim's things as soon as the police release them."

"I'd better leave before I break down and make a complete fool of myself," Sarah-who-wasn't-Sarah apologized, dropped the watch in her purse with the bracelet, and stood.

"Sometimes it can be therapeutic to let it all come out in the presence of sympathetic friends," Laura invited and wondered if the woman was capable of the acting a truly convincing breakdown would require.

"We Maxwells have always preferred to grieve in private," Sarah-not-Sarah parried. "Don't think, however, that I'm not appreciative of the thought."

"We do understand, of course," Laura said. *Oh, but did they understand!*

"Thank you ever-so much again," she said and almost ran out the door in her anxiousness to get away with her prize.

Laura leaned against the door closed between her and the fleeing woman.

"You don't know how tempted I was to blow her away," the real Sarah said, coming out of the bedroom where she'd been hiding. "If it wouldn't have gummed up everything, she wouldn't be alive for another fifty-dollar manicure."

What's more, Laura, who'd seen Sarah in action, didn't doubt the woman capable of carrying out any such threat.

"What now?" Kurt asked and scooped Laura close with his hugging arm.

"Now, I give my final thanks and get out of your lives," Sarah said. "I suspect you're anxious for some living that doesn't require looking under every rock for low-lifes."

"And you?" Laura wanted to know.

"Without Jim, I still have my faith," Sarah said. "It will see me through, as it's always seen the Jewish people through crises."

"Will we ever know how any of this turns out?" Kurt asked and pulled Laura closer.

"Probably not," Sarah candidly confessed after some thought. "Then again . . ." She gave a noncommittal shrug to complete the thought. "I do know, if you're ever in Israel, there'll always be open doors and eager arms to welcome you. Jews never forget a good turn — or a bad."

Then, she, too, was gone, Kurt and Laura, once again, alone.

"Speaking of open arms," Kurt said, and Laura moved deeper into the contentment and warmth offered by his.

"Is it over, then?" she asked and wrapped her arms around his neck.

"The way I see it, for us, the good times are just beginning," Kurt argued.

"I'll kiss to that," Laura said and, lingeringly, did just that. Oh, she relished the pyrotechnics that sparked between them!

"I love you; will you marry me?" Kurt asked when, the kiss completed, the electricity remained.

"I love you; and, of course, I'll marry you," Laura said and stood on tiptoes to better see his handsome face. "I thought you'd never ask."

"Better late than never," he said and kissed her again; Laura, submerged in wonder and pure contentment, marveled at how there still were such things as real-life, happy-ever-after endings.